DARK AND LONELY WATER

GRAEME REYNOLDS

Let the world know:
#IGotMyCLPBook!

Crystal Lake Publishing
www.CrystalLakePub.com

WELCOME
TO ANOTHER

CRYSTAL LAKE PUBLISHING
CREATION

For Charlie, Emily and Luke

My heart, my home, my family.

CHAPTER ONE

BRENDAN SIMMS GIVES the beer-soaked bar one last half-hearted wipe, then throws the sodden cloth into the sink. "That's me done now, Paul," he calls across the empty dance floor where his boss collects the evening's takings from the tills. He picks up his jacket from one of the bar stools and heads to the nightclub entrance. Brendan puts the coat on, reaching for his wallet that would ordinarily be nestled in the inside pocket, only to find it missing. He feels a surge of panic, believing for a second that it's been stolen from the staffroom. Then he remembers. *Shit!* He'd taken his wallet from his jeans and tossed it onto the bed while he got ready for work. Never picked it up again.

"Hey, Paul! Any chance you can sub me for a taxi home? I've left me fuckin wallet in the house."

His boss looks up from the till roll and shakes his head. "Sorry, Bren. Can't do it. Andrea goes off her tits if I start giving out subs. Screws the payroll right up, then I get it in the neck for the rest of the week."

It's been a long night. He enjoys this job—far more than the weekday slog at the Co-Op—but tonight had been a challenge. The club was filled with particularly obnoxious drunks all evening. Now it's after four in the morning, and all he wants to do is fall into bed beside Jimmy. Sleep until lunchtime. Brendan sighs heavily. "Can you not lend me a tenner then? It's three miles to my flat, and I'm dead on me feet."

"Sorry," Paul says. "Don't carry cash on me when I'm working. It's a nice night, though. The walk'll do you good."

Bastard. He knows that Paul is lying. He saw him fold twenty quid out of a fat roll of notes earlier to buy some weed off one of the customers. He considers calling his boss out on his bullshit but what's the point? He doesn't have the energy for the argument.

Instead, he says, "Yeah, thanks, mate. Thanks for fucking nothin. I'll just be off then?"

Paul gives a half-hearted wave without looking up as Brendan flings open the wooden double doors and storms down the stairs, muttering curses.

The evening is still warm outside the sweaty confines of the club, and a mild breeze wafts against Brendan's face. He can almost pretend that he is somewhere exotic, about to stroll along a beach instead of shuffling through the back streets of Preston. The smell makes it hard to maintain the illusion, though. The air reeks of urine, vomit, and discarded kebabs. *Ah! Preston Fishergate in the early hours of a Sunday morning. What a place. What a fucking place.*

He tries to work out the best way home on foot. He's not walked into town for literal years, and the route taken by the buses takes him miles out of his way. He'd have to walk east to the Liverpool Road bridge, then cut back on himself. The thought makes him groan. It would take him an hour at least, maybe longer. "Fuck's sake," he grumbles. It will be light by the time he gets home at this rate. Then he remembers the park. There's a footbridge over the river by Avenham Park, he thinks, with a path beyond that heads towards his estate. The map on his phone confirms it— almost a direct line—and he estimates that he can be home in half an hour. It's not the safest route, and that gives him pause. What is a generally pleasant environment during the day has a reputation of being filled with smackheads, muggers, and god-knows-what-else after the sun goes down. Brendan thinks about this for a moment, weighing the risk. *Fuck it,* he thinks. *The club kicked out almost two hours ago. Most of the pissheads will be home by now or passed out in a skip in a pool of their own puke.* Stuffing his hands in his coat pockets, he begins the walk to Avenham Park.

For the most part, the streets are silent as Brendan trudges home, the glass and steel of the darkened shop fronts and bars shifting to tightly packed rows of red-bricked terraces and empty, echoing car parks. The few people he does pass seem to either be doing the walk of shame or are so badly intoxicated that they're still lurching home. He recognises a few people from the club and nods cordially to them, but he can't be arsed to do more than that. He always makes an effort to be chatty at work, but the last thing he needs right now is to get caught up in some pisshead's blather.

His bed and his boyfriend beckon him on, urging him to pick up his pace.

Avenham Park has been given something of a facelift since his last visit. When he'd moved from Dublin to Preston as a teenager, the park had been a dark, sinister place, even during the day. Nothing but muddy footpaths and lots of secluded spots for Brendan and his friends to drink cheap cider and smoke weed when they could get it. The difference made in a few short years is quite remarkable. The muddy footpaths have been replaced with broad gravel walkways, with faux-antique streetlights dotted every 30 meters or so to banish the shadows. It's actually quite pleasant, and Brendan considers bringing Jimmy here in the afternoon—once he's caught up on his sleep. It will do Jimmy good to get away from his PlayStation for a bit, he thinks. Give them a chance to talk properly. Maybe bring a picnic and a cold bottle of prosecco. He smiles at the thought. They'd done stuff like that all the time last year, back when they started dating, but they seemed to have struggled to break out of their self-imposed winter isolation. *Well, enough of that. There's still time for them to enjoy the summer, starting this afternoon.* He relaxes as his mind wanders, his earlier concerns dissolving into happy thoughts as he makes his way through the park towards the river and home.

The quaint-looking streetlights end as he walks down the slope towards the riverside path on his way to the bridge, and he has to spend a couple of minutes letting his eyes adjust to the gloom. There is a faint glow in the sky to the east, and the dawn chorus is tuning up, with a few early-rising birds making their presence known. However, as he walks further into the darkness, the birdsong falls silent. Brendan feels a moment of unease, and he tilts his head. The only noises he hears are the gentle gurgling of the river and the soft crunch of his footsteps on the gravel path. "Lazy little sods must have decided to go back to bed for a bit," he chuckles, fighting the raw edge of his nerves. He picks up the pace, feeling his heart race a little but unable to attribute this flutter to anything concrete. "Sort your fucking head out, Bren," he mutters and begins to cut west toward the bridge.

The twinkling streetlights of the central park are still visible through the trees, and, across the river, he can see the orange glow of civilisation. *I can be home in ten minutes if I get a move on,* he thinks and begins jogging towards the bridge, all thoughts of fatigue gone for the moment. As he reaches the sloping concrete ramp which leads up to the bridge, a loud splash erupts from the river behind him. Brendan's unease erupts in a second, a geyser of adrenaline flooding his body. He tries to reassure himself, but whatever that is, it sounds a fuck-sight bigger than an otter. A swan maybe? A person? *Fuck!*

"Hello? Is there anyone there?" he calls, feeling foolish. He hasn't seen anyone else, but he needs to be sure. Some drunk might have fallen in the river, so he rushes over and calls out again.

The water erupts in a frenzy, off to the right, beneath an old weeping willow. Brendan thinks he can make out a figure there. A woman? There's a keening sound, something akin to a scream but higher-pitched, almost beyond his perception. It sets his teeth on edge and sends a finger of fear down his spine. "Hold on," he shouts, "I'm coming!"

He sprints toward the willow, dialling 999 as he does. The waters beneath the tree become still once more, the last ripples borne away by the river's current. "Fuck! Where are you," he yells, just as the call connects, and a bored metallic voice says, "999, which service do you require?"

"Yeah, my name is Brendan Simms, and I'm by the tramway bridge in Avenham Park. Preston. I've just seen a woman fall into the river."

"OK, I'm putting you through to the police. Please hold the line," says the voice on the phone.

Brendan looks back to the still surface of the river and the eddies of current swirling around beneath the branches of the tree. It would take the police at least ten minutes to get here, maybe more. That would be far too late to help the woman.

"Bollocks," he mutters, and throws his phone and shoes onto the riverbank before wading into the water. The cold shocks him as he edges his way deeper into the water. The current is pushing against him steadily, making it difficult to keep his footing, but he struggles on to the last place he saw the shape. "Hello!" he cries out, "can you hear me?" but there is no reply. He crouches down, frantically sweeping his arms through the water, but all he feels are the thick tangles of duckweed that seem to cling to his limbs and slow his movements. "Hello!" he yells once more, voice tinged with desperation. *She must have been taken by the current,* he thinks. *I'm looking in the wrong fuckin place!*

He glances downstream to where the stone pillars of the bridge rise from the rushing water and reasons that the woman may have caught herself against them. He turns around, intending to wade to the bridge, hoping he comes across her in time when a series of large air bubbles breach the water behind him in a sudden plume. Brenden turns back, hopeful, then terrified when he sees what is rising through the dark water to reach him.

He doesn't even have time to scream.

Chris Buchanan parks his ancient Range Rover as close as possible to the crime scene without crossing into the restricted area. He gets out of the vehicle and gazes down from his vantage position on top of an old stone bridge. It's a hive of activity down there, with police officers searching both downstream banks while other officers cordon off the footpaths to prevent curious onlookers from getting too close. It's only a little after six in the morning, and the sun is rising over the distant hills, casting dancing, sparkling motes of light across the surface of the river. A gathering crowd of dog walkers is being held at bay by a nervous young constable, trying to keep the scene free from contamination. Finally, he spots Sergeant Cooper down by the water's edge with the rest of his team. He sighs and begins making his way down the steep stone steps, conscious of the expensive diving equipment in the boot of his car. *Still,* he thinks, *I should probably find out the situation before I lug all of that stuff down these steps. Let's just hope no one nicks it.*

He flashes his ID to the young constable, then makes his way across to the rest of his team. "Morning, Sarge. Lads."

His boss, a man with thinning grey hair and the build of a rugby player, looks up from the paperwork and smiles. "Morning, Chris. Nice of you to join us. Did you have a nice lie-in?"

The rest of the team snigger at the comment. Chris suppresses a grin and pretends to be offended. While today is technically his day off, the Lancashire police dive unit is so small that he is always on call. There needs to be a minimum of four people on the surface for every diver in the water, five people in the case of a surface oxygen supply being required. He notes the generator and compressor set up and is relieved that he'd left all of the scuba equipment in the boot of his car. He grins at his boss. "Yeah, it was lovely. Had a nice breakfast and a hot cuppa, then I went back to bed to watch the telly. Got bored in the end and thought I'd better wander down here to see what you lot are up to." In reality, of course, his phone had woken him up. He'd felt like crap. The wine he'd drunk the night before hasn't helped, but by Christ, he'd needed it. The hangover is uncomfortable rather than debilitating, and the coffee he grabbed on the way is beginning to clear the fog. The chill of the water would finish the job.

Sergeant Cooper picks up his clipboard and turns back to Chris. "Right, let's get down to business. Mr Brendan Simms called 999 at around four thirty-five this morning, reporting that he'd seen a woman in difficulty near the bridge. Mr Simms's mobile phone was found close to the water's edge, along with his shoes, but no sign of the man or the woman otherwise. The working assumption is that he entered the river to assist her, then got swept off his feet himself. So, we're looking for up to two bodies. The chances are they're both halfway to Ireland by now, but we've got uniforms searching the riverbanks. We're checking the pools out of the direct current and the support struts of the bridge.

"So, have we done the risk assessment yet?"

Sergeant Cooper's smile returns. "Yes, we made sure that we did all of that for you while you were tucked up in bed. The water is between two and three meters deep—current running at 2 knots, with low visibility from silt. Expected hazards will be debris brought down the river, entanglement with sub-surface objects and of course the risks from the current, especially once you get close to the support struts of the bridge. We'll be doing a standard Jackstay search, starting in the pool over there by the willow tree. Can you think of anything else we should bear in mind?"

Yeah, Chris thinks. *The diver is hungover to fuck, and his Sausage and Egg McMuffin keeps repeating on him.* But he bites his tongue and shakes his head. "No, Sarge. Seems straightforward enough."

Sergeant Cooper slaps him on the shoulder. "Okay then, Sleeping Beauty, time to get your party frock on."

Chris walks over to Constable Garland, his attendant for the dive. Mike keeps his blonde hair cropped short, as if he were still in the Royal Marines, and seems to spend most of his spare time either in the gym or cave diving abroad. The last thing *he* wants to do after a week at the bottom of a canal is put his diving gear back on, but Mike seems to live for it. The younger police officer gives him a knowing grin. "Morning, Chris. I see you had a good night. Ready for the job at hand?"

Chris gives him the finger and begins climbing into the drysuit. While a standard wetsuit allows the water in, trapping a layer of it beneath the fabric to keep a diver warm, drysuits are sealed. Chris hates them. Cumbersome fucking things. You sweat like Prince Andrew at a school disco, and they don't really insulate you from the cold. They're the worst of both worlds, but you are grateful for them when you're searching potentially toxic or hazardous environments. The last time he'd had to wear one was in a septic tank, searching for a missing child. It was disgusting. The little bastard had been found later on, perfectly fine, hiding out in a friend's garden shed. The thing Chris hates about them the most though, is the damp feeling against your skin when you put them on. Logically he knows that they are cleaned and disinfected after every project. Still, he can never shake the feeling that he is slathering his body with the cold, stale sweat of the previous occupant. He suppresses a shudder as the thought crosses his mind and feels his skin breaking out in goosebumps.

Once the seals are fastened, Chris and Mike spend the next few minutes running through safety checks. Between them they ensure that the air supply is constant, the suit isn't compromised, and that the two-way radio in the helmet is operating correctly. Once they are both satisfied that everything is within acceptable parameters, Chris gives Mike the thumbs up, then he grabs the weighted jack-rope and sinks into darkness.

Chris has to catch his breath as he gets used to the cold water around him. It always takes a moment for the body to adjust to the ice-cold darkness, but that doesn't make those first seconds any easier. Visibility beneath the surface isn't as bad as he feared, though. Whilst the current from the river stirs up the silt at the bottom of the pool, it isn't anywhere near as ferocious as it would be midstream. Even as he sinks to the bottom, using the jack rope to guide him, shards of sunlight penetrate the gloom around him. He can see a good couple of feet into the murk. That could, in theory, speed up his search as he won't have to operate by touch alone. Unfortunately, the likelihood is that the bodies will have been carried downstream by now. Nevertheless, he'll still have to painstakingly cover the area, just in case. The bodies could get caught anywhere.

He pulls himself along the jack rope, sweeping his hands gently across the riverbed. Looking for bodies is the main focus, but he still needs to be alert to any other evidence that can be recovered. A weapon, for example, might indicate foul play, while a wallet or jewellery might be used to identify the other victim. The next ten minutes pass uneventfully and he reaches the weighted end of the rope. "Mike, I've finished the first pass. Get Pete or Josh to stop pissing about on Twitter and shift the weight three metres downstream, would you? I'll do the same at this end."

"Affirmative. Josh is moving the jack rope now. Having fun down there?"

"Yeah, it's like wreck-diving in the Bahamas," he says dryly. "I might come back after work and do it for fun."

Mike chuckles, and the radio cuts out, leaving Chris alone in the murky water. He hefts the weight and moves it downstream, then waits for the angle of the rope to straighten up before recommencing his fingertip search.

Chris carries on like this for another thirty minutes, searching one area then moving on to the next before something catches his eye. He calls it in.

Mike turns to his boss and yells, "Sarge, Chris thinks he's spotted something a little further out in the water. Says it's about the right size for a body, caught on something maybe. He's just leaving the line for a minute to get a closer look."

Sergeant Cooper picks up the radio. "Chris, how's it looking down there?"

After a couple of seconds, the radio crackles into life. "I think we've struck gold here, Sarge. It looks like a floater. There might even be two of them there. It's so murky. Hang on, I'll just get a little—"

The radio falls silent. Sergeant Cooper clicks the button again. "Chris? Chris, can you hear me? Over."

Mike feels fingers dance down his spine. The radios are custom built and about as reliable as they get. He's been on the diving branch for over five years now, and he can't remember a single failure in all of that time. He scans the surface for any signs of a problem, but the water's flowing steady. Shit. Something is definitely wrong.

"Lads," Mike yells, "I think Chris might be in trouble. Josh, get your gear on. Derek, check that air feed. Pete and Craig, grab that safety line and get him out of there. Now!"

The team springs into action. They have trained for eventualities like this many times, and most of them have either needed assistance or given it to colleagues in the past. They know how easily it can all go wrong. Josh begins donning his drysuit while Pete and Craig grab the long safety line and begin to pull.

"Jesus Christ!" says Pete, "The line must be caught on something. It's not budging an inch."

Derek and the Sergeant both drop their tasks and join the rest of the team on the safety rope.

"Fucking hell," says Derek, "Is it just me, or does it feel like something's pulling back?"

"It's not just you. Probably a submerged tree being pulled by the current. We need to get him out of there. Now. Put your bloody backs into it!"

The four men strain against the pull of the rope, making some headway before being pulled back toward the water. After another few seconds, the resistance disappears and the police officers fall to the ground.

"There. He's over there," says Derek, pointing to where the back of Chris's drysuit is visible on the river's surface.

The team regain their feet and drag Chris's limp body out of the water to the relative safety of the footpath. Mike begins removing his partner's helmet when he notices the red stain across his hands. "Sarge, he's bleeding. Going to need a medic."

While Mike finishes undoing Chris's helmet and pulls it free, Sergeant Cooper picks up his radio and yells, "Get those fucking paramedics down here, now! We've got an officer injured!"

Chris's eyes are wide open, and blood oozes from a string of puncture wounds that circle his upper torso. He doesn't respond to his friend at first but then he seems to register him and grabs Mike's uniform with his gloved hand. Chris stares into Mike's eyes with a look of absolute terror etched on his face, trying to speak but somehow unable to get the words past his blood-caked lips.

"Take it easy, mate. The paramedics will be here in a second.

GRAEME REYNOLDS

They'll patch you up. Until then, try to stay calm and keep still. You're safe now. Just breathe."

"You . . . you don't understand! You didn't see it!"

"I know, I know. We'll sort it out, don't worry. You just lie back and wait for the medics to patch you up."

"You didn't see what it did to me!"

Mike shakes his head. "What the fuck are you going on about?"

Chris grabs his partner, pulls him in close and looks dead into his eyes. "It was EATING ME!" he bellows before his eyes roll back and he lapses into unconsciousness.

CHAPTER TWO

THE SHOCK FORCES the air from Sam's lungs as her body reacts to the freezing water. She gasps for air and thrashes her limbs, desperately trying to stay afloat, to fight the numbness seeping through her body. She tries to cry out for help, but slips beneath the surface, just for a moment, as she opens her mouth and the stale, brackish water floods in. Sam kicks her legs in panic, gets her head above water, and coughs up the vile green liquid.

She tries to signal her mother for help, but she has her back to her, laughing and joking with Uncle Marcus, entirely oblivious. Sam tries to scream, but all she can manage is a high-pitched wheeze. Then something snags her ankle, and she vanishes beneath the surface.

It's dark in Miller's Pond, and deeper than she could have imagined. The duckweed and algae block out the weak morning sunlight. The beams dance and twirl through tiny gaps in the vegetation, but even these can't penetrate more than a few inches. Sam tries to chase the precious air bubbles upward, but her left ankle is still caught. Not just caught! Whatever it is, it's started to drag her deeper and deeper. The reality of her situation begins to sink in. Sam suddenly understands not only that she might die here, but that she is almost certainly going to. The concept strikes her like lightning, shaking her to the core of her being. She will never get to go to Sophie's party this weekend, never kiss a boy or get married. Instead, she will sink forever, cold and alone to the bottom of the pool.

Sam kicks out as hard as she can in a last, desperate attempt to free herself. Her foot connects with something substantial, driving her up towards safety. Her lungs burn, aching for air. The need to draw breath is overwhelming, but she has to break surface first or it'll be the end of her. She fights against the urge with every ounce of will, clawing up, up towards the shimmering light until she finally bursts from the water.

She can see her mother on the shoreline, her face creased in worry as she scans the surface for her missing daughter. Sam flails and cries out until her mother spots her and feels a surge of relief as she begins running along the water's edge toward her. Everything is going to be all right.

But then Sam feels something tug at the fabric of her sodden trousers, like a fish nibbling at a lure. She looks down into the dark water and sees spindly fingers curl around her leg. Sam draws a breath and screams for her mother again as she is dragged down into the depths of Miller's Pond.

Sam's eyes snap open, and she sits bolt upright in her bed, clutching her duvet in clenched fists. She gasps for a moment, unable to catch her breath, near paralysed by her nightmare. The sheet is soaked with sweat, and her cotton pyjamas cling to her body like a second skin. Still, despite her discomfort, she stays frozen in place, almost afraid to move in case something emerges from the shadows to drag her back into the depths.

After a few minutes, she manages to bring her breathing under control and then looks at her alarm clock. The green glowing numerals read 3.45 a.m. Again. She has a meeting with her boss first thing in the morning, and she needs all the sleep she can get. Sam tugs at the wet fabric plastered across her skin. Even if she can summon the energy to get out of her sodden nightclothes the chances of getting back to sleep are remote. Besides, she admits to herself, the thought of dropping off and going straight back into *that* dream is not appealing in the slightest. It has happened before, and on more occasions than she can count.

She reaches over and turns on the bedside lamp and clambers out of her bed. She throws her duvet on the floor, removes the sweat-soaked bottom sheet, then heads into her en-suite bathroom.

The harsh fluorescent light above her mirror is not kind at this time in the morning. Sam splashes water on her face and regards her reflection. Her blue eyes are bloodshot and peer out from deep, dark circles streaked with last night's eyeliner. Her skin is pale and beaded with sweat. Most of her short brown hair is plastered across her scalp, though several cowlicks do stick out at random angles. "Jesus, I look a million fucking years old," she groans. Her head begins to throb with the beginnings of what will no doubt be a memorable hangover. She drops two Alka-Seltzers into half a glass of lukewarm water from the tap and removes her pyjamas, leaving them in a heap next to the laundry basket. She winces as she downs the remedy, then puts on a fresh t-shirt and some sweatpants. That's better—marginally. However, she won't feel even remotely human again until she has a shower, some breakfast, and consumes her body weight in coffee. Probably not even then. Work is going to be a special kind of hell that morning. She hopes her boss won't be too much of a prick, although the chances are slim.

Sam checks the clock again. 4 a.m. Fuck. It's the wait that kills you. She pulls at the skin beneath one of her eyes and thinks about what she will do with the next two and a half hours. Sleep is out of the question, but she's too tired to read and really doesn't fancy watching telly. That leaves scrolling through the socials on her crappy phone, then. Just as she resigns herself to living vicariously through her friend Heidi's Instagram account, she hears soft crying from the other side of the wall. It's Julia again.

She tip-toes from the bathroom into the hallway, taking care to avoid the scattered toys, shoes and clothes that make the floor a perpetual minefield, then gently pushes open the door of the twins' bedroom.

Julia is sitting in bed, crying softly into a pillow she holds in two trembling hands. George is fast asleep. Once his head hits the pillow, he's oblivious to the world. His father was the same. The arsehole could have slept through a bomb going off in the street outside. Sam gently cursed him for the ability, lying awake as she so often did, listening to him snoring for hours on end. She feels a wave of grief well up as she looks at her son. So strong, so determined. So like his father in every way. She wipes a tear from her cheek. Brian has been in his grave for nine years now, and she still misses him terribly.

But her boy doesn't need her right now. She sits down on the bed beside Julia and strokes her temple. "What's the matter, love?"

Julia sniffles and wipes her nose across the sleeve of her pyjamas. "I had a bad dream. Really bad."

Julia's nightmares seem to come as frequently as her own. It's hard to know if she's picked up on Sam's fear of sleep or if she has her own troubles bubbling away in there. Whatever the cause, they seem to be getting worse. She leans forward and kisses the girl on the top of her head. "You know that they're just dreams, right? They can't hurt you."

Julia sniffles again. "The monster came back. And this time it . . . it . . . ate you up, mummy."

"But I'm here now. Safe and sound, sweetie. I'm not in any monster's belly. Any monster tries to do that, you know what I'll do?"

Julia shakes her head.

"If any monster tries to hurt me or either of you, I'll kick him right between the legs until his eyes cross."

Julia does not look convinced. "It wasn't a *boy* monster, silly. It was a lady monster. She had *boobs*! "

"Then that's even better. It hurts lady monsters even more, when they get kicked there. Now go back to sleep, sweetheart. I've got to drop you off with Grandma in the morning."

The girl creases her face up. "Do we *have* to go to Grandma's? It's boring there. She never lets us watch *anything* we want to. It's always *her* programmes with boring old people saying boring old things."

"I know, love, but I've got to go to work and I can only afford the holiday clubs twice a week. Now go back to sleep. Please. Mummy has to get up in a couple of hours, and she's really tired."

"Can you stay here with me, then? To stop the monster from coming back?"

Sam smiles tightly and curls up beside her daughter in the lumpy single bed, cuddling in close. "Don't worry, love. I'll keep you safe."

Julia is asleep again within minutes, but Sam cannot join her. She stares silently into the darkness until the dawn breaks, chasing away the last lingering shreds of her own nightmare.

"George, get here and get your bloody shoes on! I'm not going to tell you again," Sam yells along the corridor. They are already running late, and if she doesn't get the kids to their grandmother's in the next half hour, she'll have no chance of making her morning meeting. "George! Now!"

George shuffles out of the bedroom at a glacial pace, Sam's iPad clutched in his hands. "I'm coming," he mumbles, engrossed in his game.

Sam strides along the corridor and snatches the device from his hands. The boy looks at her with a familiar expression that swings from hurt to tumultuous rage. "What did you do that for?" he snaps. "I'd almost finished my level!"

She thrusts George's trainers at him, "Because I'm going to be late for work, and you dawdling with your nose stuck in the bloody iPad is making me later. Now put your shoes on, or you won't be allowed on it later." She turns her head towards the front door, only to find that Julia has disappeared. "Julia! Where are you?"

"I'm on the toilet," comes the muffled reply.

"Oh, for God's sake! Why didn't you go when you got up!"

Julia's voice begins to crack with the imminent onset of tears, "I didn't *need* to go then. Please don't shout at me."

Sam bites back her rising frustration and fights to calm her voice, "Alright, sweetheart, I'm sorry. Is it a number one or a number two?"

"Number two," comes the sniffled reply.

Fuck's sake. It's always the same. Every fucking time they need to leave the house. If she's honest, she's more annoyed at herself than the kids. She's had more than enough time to get them up, ready and out of the house. Regardless, time has gotten away from her. That realisation, combined with the hangover, helps damp down her frustration. Finally, she sighs and says, "OK, fine. But hurry up, and don't forget to wipe your bum!"

She turns to the door to find George's trainers still in a heap on the floor. He's picked up her iPad again while she was distracted. "Right! You can't have it tonight for that. Now *put your trainers on!* She storms into her bedroom, places the device on top of her wardrobe, well out of George's reach, then pulls her coat on. George puts on his shoes with an exaggerated slowness, his bottom lip puffed out like a balloon. The toilet flushes at last, and Julia emerges from the bathroom.

"Did you wash your hands?" she asks.

Wide-eyed, Julia turns around and dashes back into the bathroom, then reappears a second later, proudly displaying her wetted hands. Sam shakes her head and snorts, ushering the twins out of the front door.

The swollen grey clouds overhead have begun to secrete a persistent drizzle by the time Sam and the children emerge from Kensington High Street tube station. Sam tries in vain to shield her hair from the water that seems to hang in the air rather than fall properly, fearing that, by the time she makes it into the office, her neat brown bob will have turned into a frizzy mess. George is still not speaking to her and hangs back as she tries to hurry the children across the busy road while the pedestrian crossing is still flashing. Sam grabs the boy's wrist and virtually drags him along with her, keeping her hand tight around his wrist. The last thing she needs right now is another temper tantrum. They duck down a side street, pass through a small park and arrive at Janet's town-house. The older woman loathed Sam from the moment she set eyes on her, and the twelve intervening years have done little to soften her views. Janet never considered her good enough for her son, Brian, and hates her more for making her a grandmother. The older woman resents the title and insists the children call her Janet. Sam makes a point of referring to her as *Grandma* whenever she can. A tiny rebellion, but one that sparks joy.

Sam rings the bell and takes a step back, ushering the drenched children under the scant shelter of the stone entranceway. After a few minutes, Sam hears an impatient shuffling from the house. She half fancies she can smell the approaching cloud of Chanel through the heavy wooden door. Sam is convinced the old bitch drowns herself in the scent to disguise the tell-tale reek of incontinence, but so far she has failed to obtain any proof. Still, the thought of the immaculately dressed woman decked out in *Tena for Ladies* pleases her immensely.

The door swings open, and Janet regards Sam with disdain. Even this early in the morning, the woman dresses like she is attending a wedding. Expensive but gaudy, not a hair on her blue-rinsed head out of place. The cloud of perfume she carries with her would doubtless explode in a fireball if someone so much as struck a match nearby. "You're late, and my goodness, look at the state of the children! Would it kill you to carry an umbrella, Samantha? The poor dears are soaked to the skin! Go on," she gestures to the children. "Go inside and get out of those wet clothes. There are clean ones in the spare bedroom from your last visit."

Sam bites her tongue and watches the children scurry into Janet's immaculate hallway, dumping their dripping shoes and jackets in an unceremonious heap on the expensive hardwood floor. She manages to suppress a sardonic smile and says, "Thank you for having them again, Janet. It's murder getting them into the holiday clubs at the moment."

Janet rolls her eyes, "Well, if you'd be a little more organised, you wouldn't have to keep imposing on my time. I hope you've made arrangements for the next few weeks? You know I'm away on my trip."

Sam forces a little bonhomie. "No, Janet. I haven't forgotten. I haven't worked out all the details yet, but I'll manage something, I'm sure."

Janet tilts her head back a little and actually looks down her nose at Sam. "Well, make sure that you do. I won't be able to clear up any of your little messes this time. Honestly, I don't know why someone like you thought you'd be able to work *and* care for two children. It's no wonder the two of them run wild."

Sam feels a familiar rage surge from within, causing her cheeks to flush, but somehow she manages to restrain the *Go Fuck Yourself!* burning on the tip of her tongue. Instead, she says, "I'll pick them up at six. I do appreciate this. See you later, Janet." Then turns away and all but runs down the street before she says something she'll regret. *That's it*, she thinks, *I'm giving the kids a can of Red Bull before I drop them off tomorrow. See how the bitch likes that.* She smiles a little at the thought though she'll never go through with it. She can't do that to the kids. Plus, she needs to keep Janet on side for a few more years yet, or at least long enough for her to get out of her shitty job and into something that actually pays her enough to put the kids through childcare over the summer. Not that there is any prospect of that anytime soon . . . She checks her watch and swears when she sees the time.

Jason Holmes looks the epitome of an old-school newsman. He wears a creased shirt with the top two buttons hanging loose, rumpled suit trousers, scuffed shoes. Heavy glasses are perched on his bulbous nose, which he has attempted to diminish by means of a great bristling moustache. He hardly seems to notice Sam as he reads through the stack of papers in front of him, taking sporadic sucking drags on his electronic cigarette, as though he can extract more nicotine from the device by sheer lungpower. He'd been a 40-a-day smoker until recently, but his wife and doctor insisted that he give the habit up. This considerate intervention has done nothing to improve his already prickly temperament.

Sam drains the last dregs of the bitter coffee and wonders if Jason will even notice if she gets up to fetch a refill. He always pulls this crap when there's a shitty assignment to hand out. It's a classic power play to remind her who is in charge. *Cunt.* As Sam begins to plot her escape, Jason straightens the papers and pushes his thick glasses back onto the bridge of his nose.

"You're from up North somewhere, aren't you?"

Sam suppresses a sigh. Her Lancastrian accent has lost a lot of its regional twang over the years but it stands out like a sore thumb amid the predominately southern voices in the office. She smells a stitch-up. Her boss tends to use leading questions when he is about to make some decree or other, carrying the victim along his stream of thought until BAM! they're over the waterfall and it's too late to do anything about it.

"Originally, yes," She answers cautiously.

"Good, I need someone with a local perspective for this story. Have you heard of the Manchester Pusher?"

"I'm hardly local, Jason. I've lived in London since I was eighteen. I don't even go back to visit family."

Jason isn't listening to her, of course. His thought process is on rails. There's no stopping him until they reach their destination. It's how it always goes with him. Jason pushes a series of newspaper clippings across the desk toward her.

"Anyway, there have been drownings in the area for years now. A suspiciously high amount compared to the national average. Some are probably just drunks falling in the canal, but there are plenty of others less easily explained. Some of the locals think there's a serial killer shoving people into the water and watching them drown. The police aren't interested, but enough noise has been made that it's starting to attract attention. If there's something to the story, I want it. I need you to go up there and look into it for me."

Sam feels a rivulet of cold sweat trickle down between her shoulder blades, and she moves her hands beneath the table, hiding the involuntary shakes. "Jason, there's no way I can cover this. What am I supposed to do about my children? I can't just vanish up North, and I don't have anyone here to take care of them; Janet is away on some cruise for the next three weeks. Get Matthew to cover it."

Jason gives an approximation of a sympathetic smile as they near the waterfall. "You said you had family up there. They can help. I dare say it would be good for you all. The little angels can finally get to know their relations, and we're all happy."

She feels as if she is drowning again, struggling to catch her breath as it bubbles away from her. "No chance. There's a reason I've kept away for all these years."

Her boss lets out a long sigh, as though buckling under unreasonable demands. "OK, I'll tell you what I'll do. Take the kids with you, and I'll cover the cost of childcare. We can treat it as an expense. I know it's not ideal, but I need you to do this."

"Be reasonable, Jason! I can't just drag my kids halfway across the country and drop them off in some random creche in a strange city. You know how the job goes: I'll be out all hours chasing leads, and they'll be stuck on their own in a hotel room all night. It's not fair to them. Please. Send Matthew instead."

Her boss's shoulders sag, and he shifts to a more relaxed posture in his seat. "Listen, Sam, I know how hard this will be for you, but that's exactly *why* I want you to do it. You've got the background, you've got the accent, you know how it feels to face tragedy . . . "

Sam throws her hands back in disgust at this lowest of blows, but Jason pushes on regardless.

" . . . You'll be uniquely positioned to speak to the families and give the story some real emotional resonance. Matthew is a solid journalist, but his pieces don't have the heart that yours have. They don't have your soul. Look at the background notes at least, yeah? Do the research. If there's nothing to it, you'll be back in a flash."

Sam narrows her eyes, but the current's too strong. Finally, she picks up the manilla folder from the desk. "OK, I'll take a look, but I'm not promising anything. There are a *lot* of things for me to sort out before I can even begin to consider taking this on. And if we're talking expenses, you can cover the booze and therapy bills, too."

Jason sits back in his seat, a smug smile spreading across his face. "No rush. Take your time. I can wait until morning."

Heidi fills Sam's prosecco flute again, her face creasing in a scowl as Sam relates her predicament. "Well, I hope you told him to shove it up his big fat arse," she says, handing the glass to her friend.

Sam takes it and lets out a gentle sigh. "I tried, but you know what the bastard's like once he gets an idea in his head." Heidi gags. She's been on the receiving end of his advances. "Besides . . . I had a look at the notes. There might be something to it."

Heidi leans forward. "So, you're taking it on? Even with what happened to your mum?"

Sam drains half of her glass in a single mouthful. "Yeah. Because of it, actually. Facing my fears and all that. I mean, the thought of it brings me out in hives, but I can't keep slogging away at that shitty job for much longer. I need something big to get me out of there—a story to hit the nationals. Something to get me noticed. Head-hunted. I'm going to need a bigger place soon. I can't expect the kids to keep sharing a room once they hit secondary school. Can you imagine it? They argue enough as it is. And . . . oh, I don't know. There's something about this story that I can't shake. It could be the break I need."

Heidi refills Sam's glass once again, then raises her own. "Well, then, here's to bigger and better things for you. God knows it's long enough coming."

"I'll drink to that," Sam says, clinking their glasses.

"So, what are you going to do about the brats? Don't expect Janet will be thrilled at spending some quality time with her grandchildren."

"No, she's off on some cruise for three weeks. Can you believe she won it in a competition? So sodding typical. She can afford to go on holiday whenever she wants, while I can't even manage an 80's weekender at Butlins."

"You'd hate it, darling. Three weeks stuck on a boat, surrounded by people like Janet? I bet the whole place smells like a nursing home. You'd need a gas mask."

Sam laughs, "I think I'd cope with the smell if it meant three weeks lying on a sun lounger, reading my books and drinking champagne."

Heidi drains her own glass. "You'd be climbing the walls after two days, and you know it. So, what are you going to do about Julia and George?"

"Fuck knows. I don't suppose that *you* . . . ?"

"Sorry, chick. You know I love the kids, but I'm the cool, glamorous auntie. I don't do responsible adult. Besides, I'm off to Paris to cover some boring bloody fashion show at the end of the week."

Sam sighs. "Oh, poor you. Paris? At this time of the year? However will you cope?"

Heidi grins at her. "A girl's gotta do what a girl's gotta do. A face like this doesn't come cheap, you know, and I don't want my plastic surgeon to think I'm seeing someone else. He might start charging me full price."

Where Sam is fairly average in most ways—average height, average looks and build—Heidi looks like she just stepped out of the pages of a fashion magazine. Which is fair enough, Sam supposes, since she works for one. Where Sam tends to fade into the background, Heidi is always the centre of attention. It used to annoy her, but Sam kind of likes it that way now. It's just . . . easier.

Sam smirks at her friend. "Sooner or later, he's going to slip with the syringe, and you'll end up with lips like tractor tires. You know that, right? You already look fuck all like our photos from uni."

"Jealous much? Anyway," says Heidi, winking, "if you're interested, I can maybe get you a discount? Bit of botox around those crow's feet?"

Sam drains her glass. "First of all—fuck you. They give my face character. And besides, I don't think I'd be half as good at my job if I turned up to interview people with a face like a frozen chicken. Second, there's no way I can afford it on my wages. Even in whatever back-alley chop-shop you go to."

Heidi cackles in delighted outrage, but Sam's own laughter seeps away.

"Suppose I'd better start looking at childcare options in Preston, then."

"So, you're going to do it?"

"Yeah, I think I probably am. I think I have to."

CHAPTER THREE

SAM DRUMS HER fingers on the steering wheel and sighs at the line of stationary traffic snaking off into the distance. She hasn't driven along the M6 in years, yet it seems that the same old stretches of motorway are being dug up. What should have been a straightforward four-hour journey has become a seemingly endless series of roadworks and diversions that have stretched the trip to almost half as much again.

It had started off amicably enough, with the three of them crammed into the cheap, nasty hire car that the office had procured for her. The children were excited by the change of scenery and the opportunity to ride in a car rather than a stinking tube train or bus for once. However, their casual games had descended into bickering before they'd even reached the start of the motorway. After another 30 minutes of arguing, fighting and screaming, Sam let loose with some rather unmotherly language. The twins had lapsed into a sullen silence, the atmosphere in the car thick with tension. An hour later, George announced that he felt sick. Then that set Julia off, too. They'd had to make an unscheduled and expensive detour to the nearest service station when the pair of them pulled some exorcist shit, spraying their guts all over the upholstery. That had been three hours ago, and both children are now fast asleep on the back seat, the sugar rush from the extortionately priced sweets long since burned. For the first time in what feels like weeks, Sam is alone with her thoughts. Those and the lingering sour smell of vomit.

She can't rationalise the near-constant knotting in her stomach or the headaches that the mere thought of this trip brings on. Her childhood had more than its share of trauma for sure. The death of her parents when she was young, and the subsequent years spent with her cold, standoffish uncle had not been a picnic by any stretch of the imagination. However, her uncle made sure there was food on the table, a roof over her head, and whatever she needed for school. He'd never raised his hand or even his voice to her. He was, if anything, indifferent, and that was somehow worse. He provided for and took care of her as some perceived duty to his sister, but there was no familial love or warmth. No emotions of any kind, really. At eighteen, when she'd left for university, he'd barely looked up from the TV as she carried her things to the taxi. He couldn't have cared less. She was a burden he was finally free of. The charade of keeping in contact fell away soon afterwards. She's barely thought about the man in over a decade and has no intention of getting in touch while she is in the area. What would be the point? So, why does she feel so anxious about the trip? Try as she might, she has not been able to formulate a response to that question.

The traffic begins crawling forward once more. Finally, after another fifteen minutes, Sam reaches a junction and turns off the motorway. She reasons that she'll make far better time on the minor roads leading into Preston than attempting to struggle on through twenty more miles of roadworks.

The sensation of driving along once-familiar roads almost twenty years later is as unnerving as it is unreliable. For every familiar garage, church, or set of traffic lights, there seem to be two more forever changed or erased by the passage of time. A new housing estate where there had once been open fields, an old shop she'd loved either boarded up now or replaced by a hairdresser's or some bookie's. Stretches of road diverted in strange ways, or closed altogether, forcing her to retrace her route for some sense of direction. The sensation she mainly experiences, aside from frustration, is that of sadness and loss. She doesn't belong here anymore, yet she doesn't really feel like her heart lies in London either. She feels isolated. Cut off from her roots and detached from the life she's grown used to.

It is almost six o clock as she pulls the car up in front of the Bed and Breakfast that Jason's assistant has booked for her. The property next door is boarded up, with steel shutters across every window and a heavy padlock securing the front door. Nice. The front door, she notes, bears the distinctive indentation of a police battering ram. The only shop she's seen open in the neighbourhood is an off-licence. She shakes her head. This doesn't bode well. Apparently, there is a big convention in town, so accommodation is scarce. Still, this place is a new low even by Sarah's cheap-arsed standards. Jason will be thrilled when he sees how much she's saved on expenses.

Sam removes their bags from the boot and struggles up the stone steps to the front door while the children, awake but subdued, finish off their McDonalds. She rings the doorbell, then, when there is no response, rings it again, holding her finger down insistently. Her efforts are rewarded with muffled cursing and the sounds of someone stamping their way along the hallway.

When the front door swings open, Sam finds herself face to face with possibly the most disgusting individual she's ever had the displeasure of being within fifty feet of. The man wears a string vest, stretched to breaking point across his expansive gut, and a pair of stained grey jogging bottoms. Sam sincerely hopes there was yoghurt involved because the alternatives don't bear thinking about. The man's body odour is like a physical presence all its own—she can almost see it emanating in a heat haze. He scratches his ginger stubble and runs a hand through the few remaining strands of greasy hair plastered to his acne-ridden scalp.

"What the fuck do you want?" he demands.

"Erm . . . we have a reservation? Under the name of Ashlyn. Samantha Ashlyn? Are you the owner?"

The man scratches his backside and then sniffs his hand. "Naw, love. I'm the cook." He turns his back to her and yells, "Dave! Dave! There's some tart here. Says she's got a reservation or something?" A muffled response comes from somewhere inside the building, and the man grunts. "He'll be out in a minute. He's just having a shit." A lascivious expression spreads across the man's face as he looks Sam up and down, appraising her body. "Will you be staying with us long?"

I fucking doubt it, Sam thinks, but just demurs for now.

The cook attempts to suck his gut in. "Well, if you're not too busy, I could show you the sights." He winks at her. "And maybe a couple of other things as well."

Sam feels a wave of nausea bubble up. She tastes cheeseburger at the back of her throat and feels confident she'll vomit if the cook makes one more lewd suggestion. Which might actually be an improvement. Fortunately, a thin, grey-haired man emerges from a door within the property, fastening the belt on his trousers as he makes his way towards them.

The grey-haired man pushes past the cook and says, "Thanks, Rob. I'll take it from here."

Rob takes a step back and winks at Sam. "I'll see you at breakfast, then."

Sam decides in that instant that she'd rather eat from a skip than put anything Rob had a hand in preparing near her mouth.

Dave steps forward and extends his hand. "Ms Ashlyn? Nice to meet you. I hope your journey was OK?"

Sam pauses briefly before shaking Dave's hand and resolves to scrub her own the second she can get to a bathroom. She plasters on her sweetest smile and says, "It took a bit longer than we expected what with all the roadworks."

Dave nods in understanding. "Let's get you settled in your room then, so that you and your family can relax."

Sam beckons the children out of the car, and they all follow Dave down the hallway. The wallpaper is peeling, nicotine-stained, and the threadbare carpet has worn all the way through in some places. The whole B&B smells like someone spent the day boiling cabbages, seasoned with Rob-the-cook's body odour. They ascend to the first floor and come to a plywood door. Dave removes the padlock and hands it to her. "This is just for when you go out. The normal lock is broken, and it's better safe than sorry, you know. If you have anything valuable in the room." His intonation makes those last words into a question, which Sam pointedly ignores.

The door swings open to reveal a dingy room barely big enough to fit a single bed. The woodchip wallpaper is covered in tiny holes where previous occupants have picked at it. The carpet bears several large stains of indeterminate origin. The duvet cover, haphazardly thrown on the bed, is covered in cigarette burns, and the stench of stale tobacco smoke hangs heavily in the room along with another earthier, musky aroma.

"Mummy, I don't like it. It smells!" says Julia from her side.

"OK," Dave says quickly, "If you want to use the bath, you'll need to put a pound in the meter and give it about an hour for the water to heat up. It's down the hall on, first left. No shower, I'm afraid. Breakfast is from seven till nine."

Sam struggles to keep her smile in place. It's more of a rictus grin now. She thanks Dave then ushers her children into the room and closes the door.

She is going to have words with Sarah from the office tomorrow morning. Most of them no longer than four letters.

Next day, Sam stomps to the car, her face a mask of fury. Before she reaches the vehicle, she manages to compose herself, then opens the door and says, "Julia? George? Would you mind playing in that park over there for a while? Mummy needs to make a phone call."

The twins need little encouragement to risk life and limb and scurry off, overjoyed. Sam climbs into the car, waits for the kids to start climbing, and then lets herself loose. "FUCK, FUCK, FUCKING FUCKFACED FUCKER!" she screams, slamming her elbow in the door, then slapping her hands against the steering wheel of the Renault hard enough to make the horn beep. The children turn to look, so she forces a smile and waves at them. She kicks at the footwell good and hard, then fishes her phone from her handbag.

It rings four times before Sarah's cheerful London accent chimes from the speakers. "Hi, Sam! How are things going in Preston? Did you get to the hotel OK? Is it nice? Oh, and was the hire car alright? I know Jason put you down for a Renault, but my sister had one once, and she said—"

"Sarah . . . can you shut the fuck up for five bloody seconds?"

The phone goes silent. Sam can almost see Sarah's face crumple. On any other day she'd feel guilty, but the combined fuckups of the past twenty-four hours have stretched her patience to breaking point.

"Right, thank you. Now, where do I start? Firstly, yes, we got to the 'hotel' OK, but it's not actually a hotel, is it? It's a fucking doss house. I've never been anywhere this bad in my life, and I had to cover that dead heroin addict story last year. Remember that one? They found him naked and smeared in his own shit in the corner of a derelict house with no fucking roof. It was a palace compared to this place! The three of us had to cram into a single bed, Sarah, and when we woke up this morning, something had bitten the hell out of our legs. I don't know if it was fleas, or bedbugs or whatever the fuck lives in a shithole like this, but I'll be amazed if we don't come down with the plague or something."

Sarah sniffles over the phone, then meekly asks if they could exchange rooms, perhaps. She expects there's been some kind of mix up.

"Did you hear a word I just said? You haven't booked us into some quaint little B&B run by a nice old couple in the Cotswolds; it's more like a junkie's squat in no-man's-land. There's no way I'm staying there, especially not with my kids."

"Ah . . . Well, like I told you, there wasn't much else available. There are some big events going on in and around the town, and everything has been booked solid for weeks. Have you tried having a word with the owner? I'm sure he'd be able to do something."

"I told the owner where he can shove his fleapit of a B&B this morning while I loaded the kids and our stuff into the car to take them to the playgroup you booked. This, of course, brings me to my next point. They told me that someone had phoned up and cancelled the booking, and now they've given the spots to someone else."

There is a moment's silence on the other end of the line before Sarah replies, "Ah . . . "

"Yeah. So, I'm going to tell you what happens now: I'm getting in the car, and I'm driving back to London. I'll see you on tomorrow."

The silence from the other end of the line is longer this time. Then Sarah says, "Can you just hold on for a moment please, Sam? I need to speak to Jason."

The dreadful on-hold music kicks in with a selection of popular eighties hits, apparently recreated by an enthusiastic eight-year-old on a recorder. Mangled renditions of 'True Colours' by Cyndi Lauper and 'The Reflex' by Duran Duran are heard at arm's length. The massacre of 'Careless Whisper' is barely begun when Sarah returns to the phone, leaving George Michael to rest in peace.

"Erm . . . Sam?"

"Yes?"

"I'm sorry, but Jason said . . . erm . . . He said that you won't have a job to come *back* to unless you finish the assignment off."

"What the actual fuck, Sarah? Seriously? What the hell am I supposed to do? Sleep in the car? Drag the kids to the interviews with me? Perhaps the bereaved family members could tell me if they know of any decent creches in the area?"

"He did say one more thing . . . And please, don't get mad at me . . . ."

Sam's stomach flip-flops. She knows what is coming before Sarah utters the words.

"He said that you had family in the area, and that you can stay with them if the hotel's no good."

"No! No fucking way. I've not seen or spoken to the bastard for over a decade. Hell, I don't even know if my uncle's still alive."

Sarah's shrug is almost audible. Sam feels sick. There's no way out of this that she can see. Every fibre of her body wants to tell Jason where he can shove his job, but quitting is not an option. There are bills to pay, and she barely scrapes enough to cover them as it is.

Sarah seems to have developed the good sense to remain quiet during Sam's eruption, and stays that way, forcing Sam to fill the awkward silence. She lets out an exasperated sigh and accedes to the inevitable. "Fine. Tell that prick that I'll try to call on my uncle and see if he's prepared to put us up after all of these years. Temporarily. Because Sarah, I expect you to move heaven and fucking earth to find me another hotel and some actual day care. Got it?"

"Of course, Sam. I'll let you know the second we find you somewhere else. Sorry about all this."

The line goes dead before Sam can change her mind, leaving her looking at the phone as if someone had asked her to hold a turd. She checks the kids once more. George is dangling upside down from a climbing frame while Julia tries to dislodge him with a long, pointed stick. Jesus Christ.

She sits in the car for a few minutes more, trying to bring her breathing under control. Eventually, she dials a number from memory that she thought she'd never use again. After five rings, a man's voice answers with a gruff "Hello?"

Sam swallows in an attempt to lubricate her suddenly dry throat. "Uncle Marcus? It's Sam. Do you have a minute?"

Where the journey from London to Preston had felt, if anything, longer than its seven gruelling hours, the forty-five-minute trip from Preston back to Oakenclough flies by.

They journey North on a road that runs parallel to the M6 before turning east towards Bleasdale and the forest of Bowland which dominates the moors. The streetlights become further interspersed, and the houses less frequent markers along the side of the road as they enter the countryside proper. Barbed wire fences segue into drystone walls, just as rich arable fields filled with cattle make way for rough scrubby moorland dotted with sheep.

Yesterday, as Sam drove towards Preston, she'd been surprised at how much things had changed. Today the opposite is true. The area seems frozen in time. A new coat of paint might gild the odd front door, a white PVC conservatory may have been added to the rear of a two-hundred-year-old farmhouse, but otherwise everything is just as she remembers it from twenty years ago. At one time, she'd known the names of everyone in these houses and smallholdings. Some of the older folk must have died by now, but she doubts the new owners will have different surnames. That just isn't how things work around here. People didn't move away, and it is even more unusual for new people to move in when a family tree goes to rot. The house or farm is commonly abandoned and eventually reclaimed by nature, while the surrounding land gets unofficially annexed by the neighbours. She doubts whether the title plans held by the Ordnance Survey bear much resemblance to the actual boundary fencing.

The adrenaline kicks in again, her stomach flip-flopping and every instinct screams at her to turn the car around and damn the consequences. Sam slows her breathing, inhaling for three seconds and out for six, as per the stress management course. Her heart rate begins to slow, and the sick feeling in her stomach dissipates over the course of a couple of minutes. She wipes her sweaty hands on the steering wheel and lets out a long, resigned sigh. She takes the turning to Miller's Farm, the place where she spent her childhood. The place where her mother died.

She looks out across the moors to the three radio transmitters nestled on a distant hill. They light up at night, she remembers, red warnings to aircraft to prevent collisions. She always loved them. To her childhood imagination, they represented a gateway to another world, far away from this dour and lonely moorland.

The crunch of the Renault's tires on the gravel track and the subsequent rumble across the cattle grid wakes the children from their slumber. None of them slept well the previous night, so they had passed out on the back seat almost as soon as the car hit the road. Now they wipe their eyes and peer out of the windows in confusion.

"Mum?" says George, "Where are all the houses?"

"There aren't many houses around here, love. It's mostly just farms."

Julia brightens up. "Is Uncle Marcus a farmer? Does he have any lambs?"

"No, sweetheart. He used to keep some, but that was a long time ago when I was just a little girl. There will be lots of lambs around on the moors, though. We can go and see them, I'm sure."

George appeared to be thinking something through. "Mum? If there aren't any houses, will we still be able to get Domino's pizza delivered?"

"I don't know, love. We'll have to ask your uncle."

The house is almost in view now, the merest hint of it visible through the towering line of poplar trees that mark the beginning of the property. Sam feels another pang of anxiety as they approach her childhood home. The sense of travelling back in time is palpable. The place looks exactly the same as she left it all of those years ago. Even her uncle's old pickup truck, she notes. The peeling paint on the window frames and doors is the same faded, sickly shade of green.

George doesn't look impressed. "People live here? There's nothing to do!"

Sam manages a smile, despite herself. "I managed to keep myself occupied, and I lived here for nearly ten years."

"Yeah, but we aren't talking about the olden days. It's different now. If they don't have WIFI, I'm leaving!"

Sam parks the hire car next to the old truck and turns the engine off. Something has been playing on her mind all day, and she needs to get it off her chest now, before things get complicated. She turns around and fixes each of them with a serious look.

"Listen, you two. This is important. There's a pond at the back of the house, but you MUST NOT go anywhere near it. Understand?"

Julia lights up. "Does it have fish in it? Or frogs?"

"No! There's nothing like that in there. I don't think you heard me. It's dangerous, and I need you to stay from it. Far away. Got it?

Both children groan their assent and, satisfied that she's gotten through to them for once, Sam ushers them all out of the car and up to the farmhouse.

It feels strange, standing before the doorway to her former home. it doesn't seem right to just walk in after so long. So instead, she raps three times on the corroded brass doorknocker. She hears scrapes and movement from within. After a minute, the door opens and she stands face to face with her Uncle Marcus—the man who effectively raised her.

Like the property, time seems to have hardly passed for the man, even though he must be approaching his seventies by now. His stubbled chin had been salt and pepper when she'd last seen him, and the bristles are pure white now. His once thick black hair has thinned a little but otherwise he looks much the same. His muscular physique seems a little slacker, a little thinner but not unhealthily so. Only the bags beneath his eyes and a slightly jaundiced skin tone indicate the man's actual age. Sam's sense of stepping back in time is almost overwhelming.

Marcus looks her up and down. "Aye, I thought it might be you. No need to stand on ceremony here, lass. Or do they knock on their own doors down in London these days?"

"It didn't feel right, just walking in after all of this time."

"Don't talk daft. This place has always been your home, and it always will be. Treat it as such." Marcus looks down at the twins who stand behind Sam. "And who do we have here?"

Sam moves to the side and gently prevents Julia from clinging onto her. "This is George and Julia, my children. Guys, this is your Uncle Marcus."

Both children give a shy "Hello", then try to hide back behind Sam's legs.

Marcus's face spreads into a toothy grin, and he produces two chocolate bars from behind his back that he hands to the children. "We don't stand on ceremony here. You can call me Granddad if you like." He turns around and walked back into the house. "Come on in, then. Let's get you settled."

CHAPTER FOUR

SAM FOLLOWS MARCUS into the house, expecting the same dark, dingy decor she'd grown up with—the open fireplace adorned with brass ornaments, the old creme faux-fur rug, the tiny kitchen with cupboards handcrafted from plywood surrounding a rust-stained cooker—but the place has been completely remodelled. She halts in something like shock, taking it all in. The stud walls have been removed, turning the downstairs into an airy open-plan living area. A sizeable LCD TV sits in the corner, and a new log burner stands in front of the old hearth. The single lightbulb with the faded, threadbare shade she remembers from the living room is gone, replaced by tasteful LED lighting which artfully illuminates the various nooks and crannies housing family memorabilia. The house looks like a show home. Perhaps most jarring is the smell. No longer does the air reek of smoke and soot from the un-swept chimney. Instead, the farmhouse smells of air fresheners and wholesome cooking. Sam finds the disconnect rather unsettling.

Marcus's face cracks into an uncharacteristic grin. "Aye, the old place needed a bit of an update. I don't think I'd redecorated since before you were born, so I got some lads in to give it a makeover."

"It's . . . lovely, actually. Not what I expected, if I'm honest, but it's really nice."

"I've had the bathrooms and spare bedroom done too, so the littluns can set up camp there. I've not touched your room, though. Left it just how it was in case you ever needed to come home."

Sam's anxiety evaporates in the unexpected heat of shame. "Look, Marcus, I know it's been a long time since we spoke . . . ."

"Don't worry yerself over it, lass. I know you've had a lot on over the last few years, what with these two and your job. Their dad left you, did he?"

Sam doesn't know what to say, her throat suddenly dry and her mind spinning for some thread of conversation to break the sudden awkward silence.

Marcus pats her on the shoulder. "Sorry, lass. Not my business. Anyway, get your gear stowed and get yourself settled. You remember the way? Your room is at the far end of the corridor, next to my office. My room is at the top of the stairs, and the spare room is between that and the bathroom."

George tugs on Marcus's sleeve, Sam's iPad is somehow already out of the suitcase and in his hand. "Grandad Marcus—do you have wifi?"

A smile spreads across the old man's face. "Of course we do, lad; this isn't Yorkshire! The password is Samantha1983. Capital S."

Sam turns her back and hurries up the stairs with their bags before anyone spots the grateful moisture welling in her eyes.

Marcus hadn't been exaggerating when he said her room was as she'd left it. Sam vividly recalls the day she left for university, hastily stuffing her clothes and belongings into suitcases, eager to escape from the place. And look! Her old duvet is in the same crumpled heap at the foot of the bed; the drawers of her antique hardwood dresser are still out. Posters of her favourite Britpop bands still adorn the walls—faded with time and curling at the edges. She peers at a small pile of CDs on her old writing desk and flicks through a few books that she'd left behind. Marcus has obviously dusted the place; the scent of furniture polish still hangs in the air. Despite that, the room feels musty, like a museum. She walks over to the window and slides the wooden frame up to let some fresh air into the room. Her eyes fall on the stagnant water of Miller's Pond that dominates the rear of the property. Her dream comes back to her then—the sensation of drowning. Of being pulled beneath the murky waters—and Sam shudders. She draws the curtains and leaves once more, unwilling to even look at the water. She needs some air; the confines of the room suddenly claustrophobic.

Sam makes her way back downstairs again to find George and Julia sitting cross-legged on the floor. The children regard Marcus with rapt attention as he reads to them from an old leather-bound storybook. She is astonished to see her iPad discarded on the floor, forgotten. Usually, it would be welded to George's hand.

Marcus looks up from the book. "Everything alright, love?" he says.

Still shaken by the memory of her nightmare, she forces a smile. "Yeah, it's all good. Thank you again for doing this. I hate to ask, but I need to get to work. Can you keep an eye on them? I've got some people I need to interview, and I'm already running late."

"Ah, the little 'uns are no bother. I'll get dinner on about six, if that's OK?"

"That would be lovely. Thank you so much." She turns her head to the children. "Be good for your Uncle Marcus, guys, and remember what I said."

Both children roll their eyes. "Don't go near the pond," they drone in unison.

She picks up her laptop and hurries back to her car. The day has not gone anything like she'd expected, which happens to be a good thing in this case, but old anxieties remain coiled in her stomach, like a snake waiting to strike. They don't begin to fade until she puts Miller's farm far behind her.

Sam pulls the car into the driveway of the first person lined up for an interview. She'd been expecting a run-down council house or terraced property, so she is surprised at the large, well-kept detached property on the outskirts of town. The lawn is freshly mowed, borders filled with a tasteful array of flowers and plants that seem to be thriving despite the long hot summer. She checks her notes, getting the basic facts straight in her head. The victim's name is Kevin Fuller, a well-regarded middle-manager at an IT consultancy firm. No evidence or anecdotes to indicate he was anything other than a respectable man. She picks up her voice recorder and notebook from the car's front seat, checks her hair and makeup, then walks up to the front door and rings the bell.

A large dog barks furiously from somewhere inside the property, accompanied by a scolding voice. The dog's barking continues but becomes muffled as it is presumably bundled into an adjoining room. A shadow falls over the glass pane, and then the door opens to reveal a well-groomed, rather sad looking, middle-aged woman.

"Hello?" she says doubtfully, casting her eyes around to ensure that Sam is alone.

"Mrs Fuller? I'm Sam Ashlyn from News 24/7. We have an appointment?"

"Ah, yes," says the woman, some of her nervousness fading. "I was expecting you a few hours ago. I presumed you'd changed your mind."

Sam gives the woman her most apologetic smile. "Yes, I'm sorry about that. Unfortunately, I had some childcare issues that I needed to take care of."

Mrs Fuller returns her smile, albeit weakly. "Yes, I've been there. It's been a difficult few— oh, I'm sorry, where are my manners. Please, do come in."

Sam follows Mrs Fuller into the house, closing the door behind her. The house is tastefully decorated, with a solid wood floor and matching oak furniture. The walls are adorned with framed family photographs showing Mr and Mrs Fuller and their two young children."

"How old are your little ones?" Sam says, nodding to the picture.

"Four and six. They don't really understand what's happened yet. I think they still expect their dad to walk in the front door. I keep feeling that way myself. Would you like a drink?"

"A coffee would be wonderful, thank you, strong, black and two sugars, please," says Sam. The lack of sleep is catching up with her, and the bug bites along her legs are itching.

Mrs Fuller seems disappointed, as though she had another kind of drink in mind. She busies herself with a large, expensive-looking coffee machine while Sam sits at the kitchen table and looks out at the rear garden. Like the front of the house, it is immaculately maintained. The effect is only spoiled by an array of gaudy plastic toys scattered across the lawn.

When Mrs Fuller hands her the coffee cup, Sam takes a sip, relishing the flavour, and clearing her mind. She turns her voice recorder on and clears her throat.

"So, Mrs Fuller—"

"Karen," she says. "Please, call me Karen,"

"OK. Karen, I know that this will be difficult for you, but please tell me what happened in your own words."

The woman gives Sam a wan smile and takes a sip of her own

coffee before cradling the cup in her hands. "Well, Kevin always gets up— *got* up early for a run each morning. We're both so busy, you see, and what with his job and the children, he found it quite difficult to get his exercise in. So, he would get up around five-thirty for a run around the nature reserve. A good five miles! Then he'd come home, shower, and eat breakfast with us before he drove into the office. Regular as clockwork. He always used to say that if you didn't carve out time for the things you wanted to do—and stick to it—then life would fill that time up for you."

They sit for a moment in silence. Mrs Fuller is becoming visibly upset but holding it in admirably. She draws a quivering breath and continues.

"So, I heard him get up and leave the house, as usual, then I had a shower, got the children ready for their playgroup. They do play me up so. I was late making breakfast, but he still hadn't returned. I can remember wondering where he was and fretting that his eggs would be getting cold, and he *still*— I . . . I'm terribly sorry, please excuse me."

Sam waits numbly while Karen's tears gradually subside.

"I'm so dreadfully sorry, Ms Ashlyn. You'd think after this time, I would be able to control myself."

Sam takes the woman's hand, eliciting a little gasp for her presumption, but Karen does not shake her off. "It's only been a couple of weeks. Take your time. I understand how painful this must be for you."

Karen squeezes Sam's hand and gives her a half-smile, "Thank you, dear." She rallies a little and goes on. "I left a rather terse note for Kevin, then took the children to playgroup, and when I got back I saw that Kevin's car was still in the driveway and his breakfast still hadn't been touched. I thought perhaps he'd gone straight up for a shower, but he wasn't in the bathroom either."

She took a deep, shuddering breath, then continued with a brittle brightness.

"So I decided to go and look for him. He'd probably sprained his ankle or something equally silly, I supposed. I sometimes go running with him on the weekends, so I knew his route quite well. I'd gone perhaps a mile when I came across a group of people gathered on the shore of the lake. I knew straight away that something horrible had happened to him, and when I got closer, I saw Kevin floating . . . or at least I saw what was left of him . . . ."

Karen breaks down once again, and Sam waits patiently, though the next question is burning on the tip of her tongue.

"I'm sorry to have to ask this of you, Karen," she says eventually, "but I thought your husband drowned? What did you mean by the phrase 'what was left of him?'"

The look on Karen's face is one of pure anguish. "It was the water that killed him—or at least that's what the police told me—but he'd been mutilated almost beyond recognition. They . . . they still haven't found his legs." Her voice hitched up into something like a squeal. "And his face— Oh my god, his face . . . ."

Sam finishes the interview as quickly as she can. Mrs Fuller isn't really able to speak much anymore after this revelation. She sits sobbing at the kitchen table while Sam drains her coffee and lets herself out of the house. She sits in the car and tries to compose herself. *A man cut in half? The police must have called in a few bloody favours to keep that little nugget out of the press. What the hell has she stumbled into here?*

She is about to put the next interviewee's address into the sat-nav when her phone rings. The caller display reads Office.

"Sarah? Tell me you've found me another hotel."

Her boss's voice crackles through the speakers. "No, Sam, she hasn't. Get your mind on the job. I've just had a tip-off—they've found another body."

Sam parks in the public car park of Preston Moor and makes her way to the crime scene on foot. The park is quiet considering the school holidays and the nice weather. A few people are walking dogs close to a wooded area carpeted with an array of wildflowers, and some tourists are taking photographs by an observatory. It feels curiously empty. Sam soon discovers why. Crowds have begun to gather outside the police cordon, frightened people just wanting to know what has happened. A tent has been set up on the shore of the Serpentine Lake for forensics.

From where she stands, there isn't much to see; the view is obstructed by onlookers. Instead of fighting through the crowd, she makes her way around the cordon to a less congested area and approaches a pair of bored-looking constables standing watch in hi-vis jackets.

She fishes in her pockets for her press credentials and flashes the officers her best smile. "Hi," she says. "Samantha Ashlyn, News 24/7. Can I ask what happened here?"

The police officers roll their eyes, and the taller of the two, a young man in his late twenties, says, "There's been an incident, and a man's body was found in the lake. Beyond that, I'm not at liberty to say."

"Any evidence of foul play?"

The other officer steps forward. He's an older man, heavy set, with pepper-pot streaks of grey in his beard. "We really aren't at liberty to say, Ms Ashlyn. Our investigations are ongoing, and the chief will make a statement later today. I suggest you wait for that."

"So, you don't think it's linked to the Avenham Park incident a couple of weeks ago? Or the death of Kevin Fuller last month?"

The younger officer shoots his colleague a concerned glance, but the old fella isn't perturbed. "As I said, Ms Ashlyn, a statement will be issued later this afternoon once the family has been notified. It's a matter of propriety and respect."

Sam has been stonewalled plenty of times before. She knows the game. And she also knows that what the police officers don't say is just as important as what they do. She adopts an innocent look and says, "Any body parts missing? Arms or legs, maybe?"

That brings about an abrupt change in their demeanour. The younger one looks visibly shaken, and even his colleague seems surprised at the question. She pushes on, sensing she's caught them off guard. "Do you think this could be connected to the series of deaths attributed to the Manchester Pusher?"

The younger officer's face flushes, and he steps up to the cordon, towering over her. "Look, Miss, we will not speculate on any wild stories about serial killers or boogie monsters. You want to chase conspiracy theories? Go talk to Chris Buchanan. We've got actual work to be getting on with here."

Bingo, she thinks as the older officer gives his colleague a swift kick in the back of his ankle. "Chris Buchanan, you say?"

Sam parks her car in front of the building and tries to work out what she'll say to Chris Buchanan. She's dealt with her share of police officers over the years, but rarely one that wants to cooperate. A police officer suspended from work for allegedly drinking on the job is one thing, but this case seems different. She'd managed to glean a few more nuggets of information from the younger officer at the Preston Moor crime scene after the other officer needed to answer a call of nature. Namely, he'd been injured retrieving a body. His report had landed him a psychological evaluation along with the suspension. She knows police dive work is challenging and traumatic at the best of times. Chris Buchanan's testimony could simply have been a combination of the alcohol in his system, oxygen starvation, stress or any number of other factors. But there is also a chance that, by speaking to Officer Buchanan, she'll be able to start making some sense of the story because right now the pieces just don't add up.

Buchanan's building is a four-storey development of flats in a relatively new housing estate. Nevertheless, the building feels neglected. Weeds grow through the paving stones and the white paint on the door frame is flaking, exposing bare wood underneath. She looks at the list of names by the door buzzers and, on instinct, pushes three buttons adjacent to Chris Buchanan instead of his own one. After a moment, a woman's voice answers. "Hello?"

"Hi," she says, "I'm with the management company, checking on a leak in the hallway? I forgot the main key. Any chance you can buzz me in?"

Sam hears children squabbling in the background, and the woman, distracted, simply answers, "Sure," then hangs up. A couple of seconds later, the electric lock on the main entrance buzzes and Sam steps inside the building.

Chris's flat is just off the stairwell on the first floor. She takes a deep breath and knocks on the door.

A man in probably his mid-thirties, with unkept blonde hair and a stained, faded Guns N' Roses t-shirt answers the door with an attitude of deep resentment. He might have been physically attractive if not for the three-days-stubble, the red-rimmed eyes and the cocktail of body odour and stale alcohol that wafts from him.

"What?" he almost snarls.

"Chris Buchanan? My name's Sam Ashlyn. I've come a long way to speak to you. Can we have a chat?"

Chris scowls and says, "It's not a good time." He goes to close the door, but Sam sticks her foot in the gap.

"Look, Chris, I'm sure you've got a lot to be getting on with. Shaving, maybe, or showering, but this is important. I need to talk to you about the river, and what you saw in it."

Chris's mouth hangs open, a little surprised at Sam's refusal to leave. The shock soon turns to anger, however. "Which part of 'fuck off' don't you understand? I'm not interested in talking to some gutter rag reporter, especially not some rude, sarcastic bitch who turns up unannounced and starts chucking insults around. Now piss off before I lose my patience."

Sam raises her hands and moves back away from him a little, however her foot remains in place. "OK, look, I'm sorry for being a bitch. I'm not thrilled about being here either. But I'm up here looking into a series of drownings and the official story just isn't ringing true. I'd hoped that whatever you experienced might fill in some of the blanks. Maybe even help your case?"

Whatever image those words conjure, it's enough to crack his bitter resolve. Chris shrugs and steps back into the flat, leaving the door open. Sam follows, almost gagging at the smell. Stale beer, body odour and decomposing food combine to create a vinegary yet earthy aroma that makes her glad she skipped lunch. The floor and most of the seats are covered with half-empty takeaway containers, empty beer cans and discarded cigarette packets. The washing up is a lost cause, piled up like a Jenga tower.

Chris shoves an empty pizza box onto the floor and motions her to sit. "Maid's day off," he says.

Sam's smile looks more like a grimace. "I think you might want to think about sacking your maid. Pretty sure she's drinking on the job."

Chris lets out a sardonic chuckle at that. "Yeah. Her fucking attitude stinks as well. So, you said you're a reporter?"

"Yeah, I work for News 24/7."

"Never heard of it."

"Yeah. It's a small news website. Hardly fleet street level. Anyway, like I said, I'm looking into a series of drownings all across the North West that the families seem to think are linked."

Chris sits back in his chair and picks up a half-empty beer can from the floor, grimacing as he takes a swig. "What that's got to do with me?"

"Well, some of your colleagues indicated that you might have seen something odd that didn't make the press release. I want to hear all about it. Your side of things."

"Listen, I'm not fucking interested in being made to look like an idiot in my own flat, let alone in the press."

Sam sits forward. "Look, I'm not going to print your name in any story. I'm not even sure if there *is* a story yet. I'm just trying to connect the dots right now, and your insights could be critical. So, tell me, what exactly happened to you?"

"I'm not interested in having some sensationalised bullshit slapped all over the front page of some website. I'm in enough trouble as it is."

Sam nods her assent. "No problem. Like I say, I'm just trying to make sense of things. And there's a chance that if I do find something out, it could help your situation, too. I'll keep you out of any story. I promise."

Chris sighs and sits forward in his seat. "OK, fine."

"Well, I got the call out around five-thirty in the morning. Someone had made a 999 call saying they'd seen a woman in distress in the river, and then the call got cut off. When they sent a uniform to investigate, they found his phone and shoes next to the water, so they called us in to do a search."

"At first, it was a fairly straightforward fingertip search of the river bed. A team on the shore fed me air, with a reserve dive team to take over after an hour. I'd covered maybe half of the search area when I noticed what looked like a couple of bodies further out in the water, so I radioed in and went for a look."

Sam feels herself leaning forward. "Is that normal? I thought those sorts of searches were in pretty low visibility?"

"Yeah, normally, you can't see a damn thing. The sediment from the river gets kicked up by the current, so you need to mostly operate by touch. But it wasn't so bad this time around, so I had a few meters of visibility near the surface. Enough for me to see that something was going on. So, I left the rope line and started making my way over there. That was my big mistake."

Chris screws his eyes shut and takes another mouthful of his tepid beer. Sam gives him a few seconds before prompting him. "And?"

"Look, this next bit will sound fucking insane, and honestly, I don't know exactly what I saw. I had enough visibility to see the shapes of the bodies, but the water was still pretty murky,"

"I get it. Go on."

"Well, what I saw looked like two bodies—one male and one

female, locked together in the water. So, I figured that maybe Brendan Simms had tried to rescue the drowning woman; she'd panicked and drowned them both. Happens all the time. But when I got closer, the . . . thing turned her head, and looked right fucking at me. It wasn't a woman, I'll tell you that much."

"You've lost me. If it wasn't a woman, what was it?"

He shakes his head. "Fucked if I know. It fucking hissed at me, then swam right at me like a bloody shark or something. I've never seen anything move that fast underwater, especially not against the current." He shook his head in disbelief, clearly reliving the moment. His face had gone white.

"Well, it grabbed me, and then its mouth started opening and it kept on opening, way beyond what it should have been able to do. Like a snake or something, but I mean, it looked like a woman . . . "

"What happened after that?"

"The next thing I know, my fucking head and shoulders were in its mouth. I dunno how else to put it. It was trying to eat me! I must have screamed out or something, because the shore crew pulled me in. If they hadn't reacted as quickly, I think I'd have been a gonner. And that's all I can really remember until I woke up in the hospital."

Sam lets out a breath. "Well, that's a hell of a story . . . Don't take this the wrong way, but did you have a skinful the night before? Or are you sure your airline didn't get caught on something?"

"That's what everyone else thinks. Hypoxia. Hell, I'd have thought that too if it wasn't for these," Chris says, tugging his t-shirt up. "Now, you tell me, what do those look like to you?"

Sam gets to her feet and half hops over to him to study the wounds, being careful to avoid the discarded takeaways. There are dozens of puncture wounds circling Chris's upper chest and across his back in a rough shallow semi-circle, with grazes leading upwards. The marks are spaced out, a little uneven, but the pattern is unmistakable. "Well, I have to hand it to you, Chris. Those look very much like bite marks. But from what? Freshwater sharks? Do those even exist? Or are you saying you ran into a mermaid with PMT or something?"

"God knows what it was. It hurts like a bastard. The antibiotics are having a hell of a time shifting the infection it left behind, but I couldn't tell you anything more beyond the fact that it managed to bite clean through my drysuit. I don't want to think about what would have happened if the lads hadn't dragged me out when they did. It'll be a cold day in hell before I go anywhere near the water again, I can tell you."

Chris pulls his t-shirt down again, and Sam returns to her seat. "That's a bold statement considering you dive for a living."

Chris gives a bitter laugh. "Yeah, well, it's not like they'll let me carry on with that anyway once I have the psych eval and the disciplinary. I'll be lucky to get work as an admin clerk after they've got through with me."

"So, Chris, I've got to ask—before you went in there, into the river, did you know anything about the others?"

Chris's brow furrows. "What do you mean, others? You said something about some drownings earlier. What have I missed?"

Sam opens her bag and removes a sheaf of papers. "There are dozens of incidents that the victims' families think are connected, scattered all the way down the north-west coast for years. I've only just started looking into it. Still, I know of at least two others—recent ones, too. There was a guy called Kevin Fuller out for a run by a lake just south of Preston. About a week before your incident. The official report says he drowned, but they seem to have omitted the fact that both of his legs were missing when they found the body. Then there was another one this morning in the Serpentine Lake, Preston Moor Park. I don't know what happened exactly—the officers on the scene kept me away, but it seems he was missing some body parts as well."

Chris exhales and shakes his head. "I don't even know what I'm supposed to think about that. It's too much to get my head around right now."

Sam gets to her feet and says, "Listen, I've got to get back to my kids, but if you think of anything else you haven't told me, or hear anything else that might be connected, then call me. Please."

Chris takes a business card from her outstretched hand but seems lost in his thoughts. It's a lot to take in, to be fair. Sam walks to the front door, opens it and then turns back to him. "And Chris . . . maybe lay off the booze for a bit, eh?"

Chris waits for the front door to close and lets out a long breath. *They knew! The bastards made out that he was losing his mind. They fucked him over and they knew he was telling the truth!* His mind reels with the implications. *Why would they cover something like this up? Who could even organise something as big as that? And if something really is killing people all across the North West, why wouldn't they warn people? At least get them to stay clear of the water?*

He knows the answer as soon as the question forms. There is a lot of money invested in the leisure use of water in the North West. Boating, kayaking, sailing. Hell, the Lake District's entire economy is based on people travelling there for that reason. Everyone's seen fucking Jaws. He thinks of Amity's despicable Mayor and the public panic he'd hoped to quell. Shit, think about the fuss that werewolf hoax caused a few years ago. The whole damn country had been in an uproar about it until the YouTube videos were proved to be fakes. But he knows what he has seen. There's something down there. People are actually dying, and the bastards are just brushing it under the carpet. Not to mention throwing him under the bus to cover it up.

Fuck 'em, he thinks. His disciplinary hearing and psych eval are still a couple of weeks away. They'll have to change their tune if he can rub actual evidence in their faces.

Chris heads to the shower to wash away the fug of his hangover and far too many days of accumulated filth. Once he's scrubbed himself clean, he quickly dresses, then brews up a large, strong pot of coffee. He retrieves his work laptop from the bedroom and tries to log in.

Score one—his account is still active. One thing you can always rely on with the Lancashire Constabulary: nothing ever happens quickly. Apparently, that tenet takes in revoking access rights to their systems for suspended officers.

He brings up the case management system and searches for the records on Brendan Simms, the man he'd been sent down to find.

The system is old, and it takes a small eternity to retrieve the records, but then the black screen clears, and he looks for details of his last case.

The basic information is present—incident number, date, names of the recording officer, and cause of death—however, all the fine details from witness statements and the like are obscured by a single obnoxious word: Restricted.

He clears the search and tries pulling up the records for the other case Sam had mentioned. Kevin Fuller. But again he gets the same screen of basic information with the meat of the case restricted.

He begins to wonder if his access has in fact been partially revoked. Testing the theory, he calls up the details of one of his previous dives—the cesspit search for the missing child. In this instance, all of the details are there. Statements, dive logs, the whole fucking lot.

He sits back on his chair and takes a long sip of his coffee.

On a whim, he opens up Google Maps and puts a pin against the location he'd had his encounter, then labels it with the date. He drops another pin where Kevin Fuller's body had been found, again labelling it with the date. Then another at Serpentine Lake with today's date. There is a pattern beginning to form, heading north, but he has enough experience to be cautious. Patterns can be coincidental.

Chris drains his coffee and then pours himself a fresh one. He has a lot of work ahead of him.

He broadens his search parameters to show all drownings in the North West region of England in the last twelve months. The hourglass on the antique computer spins for several minutes before case numbers start populating the screen.

Chris groans and clicks on the first record. Unfortunately, he has more work to do than he thought.

In contrast to her journey that morning, Sam barely notices the drive back to Miller's Farm. She keeps repeatedly playing what Chris Buchanan told her, over in her mind. It's ridiculous, of course. The man clearly suffered some sort of mental breakdown. Still, the fact remains that people are being killed in the lakes and rivers of North West England, brutally, and the police are covering it up. She isn't ready to believe in killer mermaids or whatever other delusions Buchanan has cooked up in his alcohol-soaked mind. But *something* was happening to these people, and whatever else she may think of him, *something* had happened to Chris, too.

It is quarter to six in the evening as she crosses the cattle grid and begins the last leg of her journey down the farm track to her childhood home. She pulls the car in next to her uncle's old pickup truck and looks out at the property. So little has changed in the intervening years that she still experiences an uncomfortable sense of familiarity. The outbuildings and barns skirt the farmyard like old castle walls, despite being unused since she'd been young. Farther along the track lie the ruins of the original farmhouse which had been there since the early 1600s. The old ruins are obscured by brambles now, barely visible to the untutored eye. She was forbidden to go there as a child due to the danger posed by unstable walls and ancient rotting floorboards, not to mention the limestone caverns that dotted the hillside like swiss cheese. Of course, that hadn't very well stopped her, and she'd spent many days exploring the area and playing games amidst the rocks. Marcus had installed a steel security gate to stop her venturing into the most dangerous areas.

She gets out of the car and, suppressing the urge to knock, opens the front door to warmth and welcome.

Marcus is busy by the AGA, preparing a meal that sends another wave of nostalgia through her. Stewed beef with dumplings was one of her uncle's stalwart dinner choices when she was a child and judging by the thick meaty smell emanating from the pans, he hasn't changed his recipe much in the intervening years.

He looks up from his preparations and says, "Alright, love? Good day at the office? I've made you your favourite. It'll be ready in a few minutes."

She smiles at the old man, "I thought I recognised the smell. How are the kids? Behaving themselves, I hope?"

"They've been no bother at all. Good as gold, the pair of them. Young George has been on his devices for most of the day, and I picked up a colouring book and some pens for Julia when I popped into the village for some stuff."

"That's good. Thank you. Don't take any grief from them. I'm just going to get changed before dinner if that's OK?"

She dumps her bags in the living room and says hello to George, who grunts a response, too engrossed in his game to really register her presence. Sam heads up the stairs and sticks her head around the door of the bedroom Marcus has set aside for the twins.

Julia is sitting cross-legged on the floor, carefully colouring in a picture of a fairy-tale scene.

"Is her skin supposed to be green?" she asks her daughter. "Or is she supposed to be She-Hulk? Or Gamora maybe?"

Julia beams at her. "No, silly. It's Princess Jenna. From Grandad Marcus's stories?"

Sam frowns. The name seems familiar, but she can't remember Marcus ever reading her any stories as a child for the life of her. She feels a momentary pang of jealousy, and that surprises her. Marcus is treating her children better than he ever treated her. She recalls the cold indifference of the man in the years they lived together. It always felt like he was keeping her at arm's length; like he didn't want to get to know his niece, let alone care for her. *Perhaps people do change,* she thinks.

"I don't know that particular story, sweetie. You'll have to tell it to me later on. I wanted to let you know that dinner will be ready in a few minutes, so make sure you wash your hands."

Julia gives Sam another glowing smile. "I will, Mummy. Hey, Mummy! Do you like our room?"

Sam hasn't really paid it much attention, but she takes it in now. The surprises keep coming. When she'd been a child, this had simply been a dumping space for boxes of old junk. It has been completely renovated recently, by the looks of it, with bunk beds, a deep pile carpet, and walls painted a light sage colour. There are photographs of the farm and surrounding area hanging on the walls, framed nicely. Hah! There are even a pair of cuddly toys in each bed, nestled within the new duvet covers—Spiderman on George's Bed and The Powerpuff Girls on Julia's.

"It's lovely. Make sure you thank Grandad Marcus for making you such a lovely room."

Sam turns back towards her own room and can't help but wonder why Marcus has gone to the trouble of sorting out a kid's room. She'd not known that she was coming here until that morning, and she'd not spoken to or contacted Marcus in years— certainly not since the children were born. Yet the fact that he had two grand-nieces and nephews not only didn't faze him when she'd brought it up but there was a room ready for them.

She shakes off the thought, resolving to speak to Marcus later about it, and opens her suitcase, rooting through it for something comfortable and casual for the evening. She makes her way downstairs to find both children sitting at the old pine farmhouse table, the only original pieces of furniture in evidence. Marcus places the steaming pot of stew in the middle of the table and ladles out portions into each of the children's bowls.

George screws up his face as he examines his dinner, pushing things around the bowl with his spoon. "There are VEGETABLES in this!" he says, giving his sister a horrified look. Sam had been expecting this reaction with a mixture of embarrassed dread and private glee. Neither of the children are keen on anything new, unless it's deep-fried or covered in sugar. George, in particular, treats anything even vaguely plant-based with disgust.

"Now, George," she says, "Marcus has been working really hard on your dinner, so don't be rude."

"Aye, lad," says Marcus. "You listen to your mother. I'll tell you what: eat it all up, and there'll be ice cream for afters. But only if you eat it all, mind. Otherwise, your sister and mum can have all the ice cream, and guess what you'll have for breakfast? What's left of your stew."

George doesn't look convinced by the promise or phased by the threat. Instead, he pushes the globules of meat and veg around with his spoon. "Can't we just order a pizza or something?"

Marcus chuckles. "There's nothing like that around here, lad. You're in the countryside now. You need proper food to make you grow up big and strong."

George's mouth falls open and his eyes widen in horror. "No pizza? Not even a KFC? Please tell me you're joking."

Sam fails to suppress a snigger, so she turns her face to Julia in an effort to hide it. Her daughter is shovelling big mouthfuls of the stew into her mouth. The girl beams up at the old man and says, "Thank you, Grandad Marcus. It's lovely," before sending her mother a furtive glance that indicates otherwise. "Um. Grandad Marcus . . . What kind of ice cream do we have for dessert?"

"It's mint choc chip," he says. "Do you like mint choc chip?"

Julia's smile broadens. "It's my favourite! And George's, too."

George seems to weigh up the pros and cons of this new information. It's a powerful argument. Reluctantly, he begins taking small spoonfuls of the stew up to his mouth. Judging by his expression, he feels as though he is being forced to eat poison.

Sam relishes the familiar flavours and aroma as she starts tucking into her own meal. "So, Marcus, I saw the children's bedroom, and I have to say I'm impressed. When did you do all of that? And more to the point, why? Are you intending to adopt or something?"

"Oh, I got the builders to sort the bedroom out at the same time as I got the kitchen done. My mate Will comes over with his littluns on occasion, so they bed down up there if we're having a late one. Lucky really, all things considered."

"Definitely lucky for us. I can't thank you enough, Marcus. Really. You got us out of a hole today."

"If I'd known you were coming, I'd have gotten a few more bits and pieces in. Do you know how long you'll be staying?"

"Not too long, I hope. Work is still trying to find me a hotel and some professional childcare; I'm just waiting to hear back from them."

A shadow crosses the old man's face, just for a moment, and Sam feels a surge of guilt. "Well, just so it's clear, you're all most welcome to stay here as long as you like. As I said before, this is your home as much as mine. The littluns too, as far as I'm concerned. I'd love to get to know them, and to catch up with you properly, too. I understand if you'd rather stay in a Holiday Inn or something, but it's no bother to me having you here. Truth be told, I'm glad of the company. I don't get too many visitors these days. It's lovely to have some life back in the old place."

"Can we stay here, mum? Pleeease?" says Julia. "Grandad Marcus is waaaaaay nicer than Grandma Janet."

Sam looks from Julia to George and then to Marcus, feeling suddenly ganged up on. Don't they know how she feels about this place? What she went through!? Marcus does, of course, which is why he looks so sheepish, but the kids . . . Well, she's never really spoken to them about it. It's her own damned fault. Against her better judgement, she sighs and says, "OK. Fine. We'll stay here while I'm covering this story. If you're sure, Marcus. I don't want to cause any trouble."

Marcus reaches over the table and takes her hand. "No trouble at all, love. It's nice to have you back where you belong."

Sam smiles back at her uncle, though her stomach clenches at his words. *Back where I belong? Christ, anything but that.* She takes another mouthful of stew, but the food tastes strange to her now. Alien, as if somehow the familiar meal had been replaced between mouthfuls. "So, I'm intrigued, Marcus. What have you been up to? You're obviously still in pretty good shape. Have you been doing anything with the farm?"

"Not much, beyond maintaining the boundaries, if I'm honest. Colin down the valley rents the fields out for his sheep, so that brings in a little cash. I'm always having to patch up holes in the fences, especially with the young 'uns. If there's a gap in the hedge, or some rocks down on a wall, those bloody lambs'll find it, as you know. I swear I end up spending half of spring trying to catch the little buggers again."

Julia sits up, suddenly interested in the conversation. "Are there any lambs here now, Grandad Marcus?"

The old man laughs. "Not unless you're on about the bits in your bowl, love, no. Most of 'em have gone to slaughter by now. The meat in your stew was one of the last ones running around the fields a few weeks back. Colin always fills my freezer up afterwards, bless him."

Julia's jaw falls open in a horrified gape. She pushes her bowl away as though she'd discovered a rat in it. Sam doesn't know whether to laugh or be annoyed on her daughter's behalf. It seems Julia hasn't quite understood the whole farm to fork process. Every day brings its lessons. She doubts if even mint choc chip ice cream will be enough to get the girl to finish it. George, on the other hand, is tucking into the stew with gusto now, although Sam can't help but notice the growing pile of vegetables perched on the side of his bowl. She decides not to push the matter and turns back to Marcus.

"So, what else have you been doing with your time then? It must be pretty quiet up here on your own?"

"Oh, it's not so bad, love. I've got my books, of course. You know I always loved to read. And since I got the internet in up here I've got plenty to keep me occupied. I do quite a lot of online courses, for one thing. You can't teach an old dog new tricks, they say, but I don't reckon that's true if the old dog wants to do it. I've learned all sorts. And of course, I like a spot of telly. I've never been bored, don't you fret. What about you, eh? What have you been doing with yourself? For fun, I mean."

Sam shrugs. "Not much to say, really. Between taking care of these two and slogging away at the day job, I don't get much more than five minutes to myself. I see my mates from Uni sometimes, but most days by the time I've gotten in, fed the kids and had a shower, I'm about ready for bed."

Marcus shakes his head, "That's no way to live, love. I'm sorry to hear that. Truly I am. I'd hoped when you left that you'd get out into the world. Experience everything it had to offer. Live a little while you still can."

"Well," she says, unable to keep the tone from her voice. "That was the plan, but Brian had his accident while I was pregnant with these two, and that all went out the window. Any chance I had of leading my own life sort of died with their father."

George stands up suddenly and pushes his plate away. "You're saying it's *our* fault, just because your life is rubbish?"

Sam shakes her head incredulously. "No, sweetheart. That's not what I'm saying at all. What I meant is—"

"Well, I hate you, too!" yells George, and runs from the kitchen, his footsteps like thunder up the stairs, followed by the slamming of his bedroom door.

"Shit," hisses Sam, pushing her chair back to follow him.

Marcus puts his hand on hers. "I'd leave him for a bit, love. Let him cool off. I've seen it before. My mate Will's young 'uns are the same age. Don't worry, I'll have a word with him later after he's calmed down a bit."

Sam lets out a long sigh and sits back down. The rest of the meal tastes like ashes in her mouth, and no one speaks until after the plates are washed up and put away tidy. What a miserable end to the day.

CHAPTER FIVE

SAM STANDS BESIDE Miller's Pond, gazing into the murky water. The surface is covered in duckweed. The greenery stretches across the water, suffocating the pond, making it stagnant and stinky. It's a warm summer's day, and she can see her mother and Uncle Marcus walking back towards the farmhouse, laughing at some shared joke.

She picks up a rock and throws it into the water, taking some satisfaction at the splash and the hole she's punched in the green carpet of vegetation. The ripples quickly subside and the thick mass of weeds closes again, reclaiming the section of clear water that she'd made. She selects another rock, but as she bends down she realises something is wrong.

Sam looks down at her long arms, her painted nails, the boobs hanging down from her chest. She is an adult, but that's mad because she remembers this day. She was—is—only eight. Yet here she is, wearing the clothes she drove up from London in.

She takes a hesitant step away from the water, knowing what comes next. Her foot slips on the muddy shore, just as it did before, and her foot plunges into the cold, brackish water.

Sam scrambles in the mud, keeping her panic down, trying to pull herself clear, but the duckweed seems to wrap around her ankle, holding her fast. Then, to her horror, she sees five long, spindly fingers emerge from the water, clasp her ankle and start to drag her into Miller's Pond.

She screams out to her mother and uncle, who turn from their conversation, still laughing. They wave at her, unable to see her distress. Or perhaps they're entertained by it. She digs her fingers into the mud and thrashes to escape, leaving furrows in the filth, but her efforts achieve next to nothing. Slowly and inevitably, howling in terror, flailing to catch hold of something, Sam is pulled beneath the surface.

The duckweed closes above her, hiding the evidence of her passing. Only a few shifting shards of sunlight can penetrate the gloom through the green mat. She looks down and sees what manner of thing has caught her in its grasp. A woman's face leers up at her, green hair flowing in the water, pond slime draped across her flesh like a diaphanous robe, her mouth filled with sharp, bright fangs. A mouth that is opening towards her like a snake's, wider and wider, closer and closer until the gaping chasm is all she can see . . . .

Sam wakes up, thrashing at the duvet, a scream barely held in check. Once the heavy covering is safely deposited on the floor, she lies back in her childhood bed and tries to get her breathing under control. She waits in the darkness for the pounding in her chest to subside, listening out for signs that the children have been disturbed. She'd woken Julia up on more than one occasion with her nightmares, after all. Fortunately, the only sounds she hears this evening are the familiar creaks of the old house as the pipes cool.

These fucking dreams are becoming a real problem. It doesn't take a genius to work out the source of tonight's nightmare, amplified by the ravings of Chris Buchanan. This one was bad, though. One of the worst she's ever experienced. She's not religious in any meaningful way, but she prays that the new additions to her nightmare are just temporary things, brought on by her present circumstances. If they carry on like this, she'll have to make an appointment to see the psychologist again, soon! That's not a thought that she relishes. Sam is a firm believer that people bury these things for a reason. To her mind, stirring up all those suppressed memories causes nothing but pain and more trauma. No. Her subconscious is like Miller's Pond. Best left alone, and untouched. Whatever waits below, in those dark and lonely waters, can fucking well stay there.

She climbs out of bed, tugging the clammy material away from her body in disgust, and forces herself to go to the window. She pulls open the curtains and gazes down at the black, mirror-like surface of the pond—featureless but for duckweed around its periphery and the moon reflected on its surface. "You won't beat me, you fucker!" she says, feeling her lips curl up into a snarl. *The pond is just a hole in the ground, filled with water. Nothing more. Is it normal to loathe an inanimate object? Is there something wrong with her?* Still, her revulsion is real. The skin of her arms crawls with gooseflesh at the sight of it. It claimed her mother's life when she was eight years old and has haunted her nightmares ever since. *Yes*, she decides. *It is an entirely reasonable way to feel.* Honestly, she doesn't know why Marcus didn't fill the bastard thing in after the accident.

A glimmer of light on the moor catches her eye, and she peers through the glass, watching the bright spot dance across the inky-black landscape. Someone is out there with a torch. She checks her watch and sees that it is almost two-thirty in the morning. *What the hell is someone doing out there at this time of night?*

She decides that she'd rather not know the answer to this and, giving the dark waters of the pond one last glare, she draws her curtains. It takes Sam over an hour to fall back to sleep, and if she dreams again they fade like wisps of smoke by the morning.

Sam wakes up feeling as if she hasn't slept for a month. The passage of time has helped her to forget just how bloody uncomfortable her old bed was, or perhaps it's just the rigours of age. She's groggy and disoriented at first when her eyes open. The sight of her old, faded Oasis and Elastica posters makes her feel perhaps she is still dreaming, or perhaps her life as a mother was the dream, and she is still a troubled teen, wishing herself away from this place. Either way, she could do with a fresh start. It takes a few moments for her mind to catch up with the previous day's events. *Post-apocalyptic B&B. Playgroup placement cancelled. Miller's Farm and the reformation of Uncle Marcus. Right.*

She stumbles to the bathroom and has a quick shower, letting the hot water wash away at least some of her fatigue while she mentally tries to plan her day. She's read the notes for each of her visits, but runs over the broad details again, formulating the approach she intends to take with each family. Then she dresses for work and walks down the narrow staircase to the kitchen.

Marcus greets her with a cheerful "Afternoon, Sleepyhead!" which sets her teeth on edge. Marcus still apparently wakes up with the dawn—a habit developed through decades of farming.

She manages a weak smile. "Morning, Marcus," she says. "Don't suppose there's any coffee on the go?"

"There's a fresh pot on. Won't be up to your London standards, I dare say, but it's hot and it's strong."

Sam smiles gratefully, letting the jibe pass, and pours herself a steaming mug. "I'm sure it will be fine."

She sits at the table and notices, to her surprise, that the twins are watching TV in the living room. It's rare to see either of them during the school holidays before noon. "Have they been up long?" she asks.

"Oh, just an hour or so. They've already had their breakfast. Thought I'd take them for a walk across the moor later on if that's OK with you?"

Sam stumbles over that thought, then sets her concerns to the side. Dour as her own childhood was, she never felt threatened by the wild moors or by Marcus. Only the pond.

"Yeah, that's fine," she says with brittle cheer. "I've got to drive to Manchester for some more interviews. I'm not sure when I'll be back, so don't worry about feeding me tonight."

Marcus slides a plate of bacon and eggs before her, then collects his own breakfast and sits down opposite her. "Not a problem, love. I'll make sure the littluns get fed and watered, and I'll stick something in the fridge for you if you're still peckish when you get back."

"I don't suppose . . . Did you get a chance to talk to George at all?" Sam asks, avoiding her uncle's eyes.

"I had a word with him, aye. Man to man. He's fine. He understands you didn't mean it the way he thought."

Sam lets out a breath that she's not been aware she was holding and says, "Thank you. I wasn't looking forward to one of his moods this morning. He can hold a grudge like no one I've ever met." As she takes a sip of her coffee, another question that's been bothering her comes to mind. She doesn't want to hammer him, so she lets it roll around her head for a while, enjoying the taste and texture of her meal. As she sops up the last drips of yolk, she asks it casually. "I thought I saw someone out on the moor last night with a torch. Too late for a hiker. Any idea who it might have been?"

He grunts and shakes his head. "No idea. Probably one of the lads from the village, poaching rabbits. They zap 'em in the eyes with their torch, then smack them over the head while they're blinded. Daft buggers should be careful out there. Loads of potholes and caves out on the moor. Whole place is like a swiss-cheese. One wrong step, and whoosh! Down they go. Been more than a couple disappeared like that over the years."

Sam feels a pang of concern. "Are you sure it's a good idea to take the kids out there, then?"

"Of course. I know this place like the back of my hand. There's no nook or cranny that I don't know. Don't fret, girl. I'll take good care of them. Unless you'd rather we did something else?"

Sam is far from satisfied with the answer but doesn't want to push the subject. The last thing she wants to do right now is get into a fight with her uncle. Not when she has no place left to go. There has, however, been something else on her mind.

"No, I'm sure they'll be fine with you," she says with some reluctance, "But I did want to ask how come you didn't fill the pond in? You know, after what happened to mum."

The old man's face creases in sorrow. "I tried, lass. You must know that. I sent fourteen ton of rock into that thing when your mum passed, and it didn't make a blind bit of difference. Didn't even raise the water level. I reckon it's fed by those limestone caves what run through the moor, straight from the aquifer. The water level never drops, even in a hot summer like this one. For a long time after, I couldn't even look at it, but then I reckon I got used to it. That pond is a part of this place, just like me. Could have boarded over it, I suppose, but it didn't seem right somehow. Like I was walling her in. And once you left, there didn't seem much point. I suppose I should have a think about doing that now, if the little 'uns are going to be here for any length of time. Just to be safe, like."

Sam's stomach flips and she almost tells Marcus that she'd like nothing better than to see the damn thing sealed off. Instead, she shakes her head and says, "I appreciate the offer, but we'll only be here a few more days so it's not worth the effort and expense. Just don't let them out of your sight. They can be pretty wilful when they get an idea in their heads."

"No worries, love. I'll keep a close eye on them. I don't think we need to worry much, though. Neither of them have gone anywhere near it so far."

She reaches across the table and gives her uncle's hand a squeeze. "Thank you, Marcus."

Sam finishes her food, drains her coffee's last dregs, then gets up and walks towards the front door. "Bye, kids! Be good," she calls. Neither of the children even bother to turn around. Sam shakes her head and leaves the house, feeling the previous day's unease sitting in her stomach like a lead weight. *That's just the way kids are,* she tells herself. *They get to an age, and they don't need their mum anymore.* As she drives away, though, she is aware that she's lying to herself but can't for the life of her understand why.

Sam gets out of her car and walks across the street to the corner shop. Her head is throbbing with stress, lack of sleep and too much caffeine. It is not a good combination. She's all too aware that her nerves are frayed, and she wasn't half as present as she should have been in the two interviews she's just conducted. She pushes open the door and edges past a pensioner who is deep in conversation with the cashier and happens to be blocking most of the entrance. In or out, you old bag, she thinks. Some of us have got lives to lead.

Two aisles run the length of the premises. A refrigerator stocked with milk, soft drinks, white wine (and some suspiciously soggy-looking sandwiches) takes up around half the shelf space on the right-hand side. The other shelves seem to be stocked in a haphazard manner with no logic or reason to the layout. Toiletries sit alongside pasta sauce packet mixes; vegetables share shelf space with cleaning products; confectionary is shoved onto a shelf with nappies and baby formula. She glances at the cashier, trapped in conversation with the elderly lady. The poor sod is nodding agreement but wears an expression that suggests a bullet to the head may be preferable.

After some searching, she finds the painkillers tucked away behind some shoe polish. Because of course they are. She takes two packets and a bottle of water from the shelves, then, after a moment's reflection, she adds a bottle of white wine to her basket. For later.

She stands behind the old lady for three or four minutes as she yammers on, oblivious to her presence. Eventually, she can't take it anymore and leans in. "Excuse me, do you mind if I pay for these? I've got somewhere I need to be. Maybe finish your chat later?"

The woman huffs and stomps out of the shop, slamming the door behind her. Sam gives the cashier a sheepish grin. "Sorry for interrupting."

"Christ, don't apologise. She's been talking my ear off for twenty minutes. I think she'd have carried on if I dropped dead in front of her. She lost her daughter recently, love her. I think she just comes in for some company, but by heck, it does your head in after a while."

Sam pays for her shopping and dry-swallows two of the paracetamol before she's left out of the shop, wincing at the harsh chemical taste. She's about to head off to her next appointment when her phone rings. She retrieves the phone and sighs. It's Jason. *Just what I fucking need.* She accepts the call anyway.

"Hi Boss," she says with an exaggerated chirpiness that she knows will irritate him. "To what do I owe the pleasure."

"Just checking in to see how the interviews are going. Any updates?"

"Nothing conclusive. Both of the deceased were young lads, out of their skulls according to the blood-alcohol levels in the coroner's report. I swear, one of them would have died of alcohol poisoning if he hadn't ended up in the Manchester Ship Canal first."

"Hmm," Jason's voice crackles through the earpiece. "So, you think it's a waste of time?"

"I don't know. Maybe not. One of the ones I talked to yesterday was about as far away from a drowning as you can get. Cut in half from what the wife said. Same with the one at Preston Moor Park. The police are keeping a pretty tight lid on things, though. I did speak to a police diver who's on suspension, but I couldn't get much useful information out of him. Bit of a drunk, I think, and on the verge of a nervous breakdown."

"OK. Well, keep digging and let me know if you turn anything else up."

Her boss hangs up before she has a chance to say anything else. She suspects he's trying to avoid any further questions about accommodation or day-care for the kids. *Cheap bastard.* She's not going to give him the satisfaction of hearing that things are actually going alright with Marcus at the farm. She is, however, putting her bottle of Pinot Grigio on her expenses claim.

Her next appointment is only three streets away from where she's parked, so she decides to walk. The day is warm and pleasant, with a cool breeze that makes the flowers of a nearby magnolia tree dance on their branches. Her headache is finally starting to fade, and, despite her tiredness, Sam feels her mood begin to improve. The area is quite pleasant, really. Each street is made up of neat rows of red-bricked terraced houses. Most of the properties still have their front gardens, well maintained, bright and colourful. Whilst some houses have converted their gardens to driveways, they act as punctuation rather than spoiling the feel of the place. A group of four young children are playing in the street, the sight of which brings a smile to Sam's face. It's quite rare to see kids outside these days, enjoying the sunshine. She can't remember the last time she saw her children entertaining themselves without a screen being involved. She decides that she needs to try to get George and Julia outside more. Perhaps the walk on the moor with Marcus might kindle a new-found love of fresh air and the outdoors, although she doubts it. Sam turns right onto the street she wants, finds the house she's looking for, then rings the bell.

Then the door swings open. Shit! Facing her is the pensioner from the corner shop.

The woman looks her up and down with a look of distaste, bordering on contempt. "I suppose you're the reporter, then?"

"Samantha Ashlyn from News 24/7, yes. Pleased to meet you, Mrs Boswell," Sam says, extending her hand.

The woman doesn't take it. "Well, what are you standing out there for? You're letting all the heat out. Come in, and make sure you leave your shoes by the door. I've just swept up, and I don't want you trailing muck through the house."

Sam hurries after her into what initially feels like a sauna. The temperature must be close to ninety degrees. Sam puts her hand against the radiator in the hallway and withdraws it immediately with a yelp of pain. She follows Mrs Boswell into a neat sitting room, filled with dozens of statuettes of clowns adorning every surface. She sits opposite the older woman, blustering an apology. "Mrs Boswell, I am so sorry if I offended you earlier. I was a little sharp, but that was only because I didn't want to be late for our appointment. If I'd known—"

Mrs Boswell raises a hand to stop her. "Never mind. What's done is done. I did think you rude at the time, but at least you've apologised for it, I'll give you that. Too many people think they're above apologies these days. Manners cost nothing, nor common courtesy. Speaking of which, would you like a cup of tea?"

The last thing Sam wants is a hot drink in this sweltering heat, but she doesn't want to offend the woman any further. "That would be lovely, Mrs Boswell. Thank you. Milk please, no sugar."

Mrs Boswell smiles for the first time and says, "Call me Mabel. Make yourself at home, and I'll be right back." She heaves herself up from her high-backed seat with obvious effort and shuffles out of the room, leaving Sam alone.

Sam looks around the room and suppresses a shudder. There are clowns everywhere. Four figurines sit on top of an ancient television in a walnut cabinet, with two more in the cabinet itself. The gas fireplace sports an array of them, carefully arranged so their respective antics appear to be part of a circus performance. A glass display case sits behind a corner sofa, and it too is packed with the painted monstrosities. There is a portrait of a classical clown above the fire, and even the cushions on the sofa continue the garish motif. The effect is unpleasant and deeply unsettling.

"I see you're admiring my collection," says Mrs Boswell as she enters the room. She hands Sam a cup of weak, grey tea and sits back in her chair.

"Er, yes. It's certainly very . . . colourful," she replies.

"Thank you," says Mrs Boswell, taking Sam's comment as a compliment. "Sarah hated them. She said they 'gave her the ick', whatever that means, but I think there's nothing brings a smile like a clown. And goodness knows, we can all do with something to smile about these days . . . "

Sam takes a sip of her tea and immediately wishes she hadn't. The dominant flavour is that of lemon scented washing up liquid. She puts it down beside her and says, "Sarah? That's your daughter, yes? Can you tell me what happened to her?"

Mabel's face crumples, she lets out a loud sniff and then wipes her nose on her sleeve. "She was such a good girl. Always here to take care of her old mum. I couldn't believe it when the policeman came to the door to tell me they'd found her. In the canal of all places. It broke my heart."

Sam puts on her best sympathetic expression and says, "I'm so sorry for your loss. Did the police say what they thought happened to her?"

"Pfff! Those useless buggers don't know a bloody thing. Said she'd filled her pockets and bag with bricks and jumped right in. Even say they found a suicide note on her, but I don't believe that. Not for a second. Not my Sarah."

"Why do you think that? If there was a note, I mean."

"I saw her that morning, and she was fine. Just normal like

always. And she had no reason to do something so stupid, so selfish. No. The only thing that makes sense is that someone forced her to write those horrible things before they killed her. Some people are just sick."

Sam shuffles uncomfortably in her seat. "Horrible things?"

"Yes. Awful things in that note. About me, mostly. Saying she can't stand it anymore. Can't deal with my interfering in her life— as if I'd do that. That Neil she was seeing was up to no good an' all, and she knew it deep down. All nonsense. I'd bet money that good for nothing little shit was responsible one way or another."

Something inside Sam sinks, though she masks it well. Another dead end, then. And based on what she'd seen in the shop, Mabel Boswell is just getting warmed up. Sam focuses on her breathing, keeping herself neutral, allowing the woman to unburden herself. The bereaved always search for some reason or explanation for the death of a loved one. God knows she spent long enough looking for one after her mother drowned. And poor Brian. Mrs Boswell's story may not be the one she was hoping for, but she will let the woman say all she needs to. To do anything else would be cruel.

Sam lets her talk for another fifteen minutes that flow like molasses, until she feels that she's done her duty to the old lady. She'd already started repeating herself, going back over the same sections of the story over and over again, so Sam decides she can excuse herself without appearing rude.

"Thank you, Mrs Boswell. I think I have all I need for now. If I have any other questions, my office will give you a call."

Mrs Boswell shakes her head. "Nonsense. You've not finished your tea, and I've not finished telling you about her yet. Here, let me get the photo album too in case you need a picture for your story . . . "

It is almost four in the afternoon when Sam parks up for her last interview. She massages her temples and shoulders, weighing up whether she should push on or just cancel and head back to Marcus's. She'd been stuck in Mrs Boswell's house for over two hours, sweating in the centrally heated hell while the old lady had gone through old pictures and shared anecdotes about her daughter. Sam had dutifully taken notes, which she screwed up into a ball and threw in the footwell of her Renault the second she made it back to the car. Then she drove to her final interview of the day in the Moss Side council estate.

Moss Side is legendary for all the wrong reasons. According to the papers, it's a lawless wasteland. The burned-out car in the middle of the estate's central roundabout is testament to its shitty reputation, as are the graffiti-splashed steel shutters across the windows and doors of the shops, but there don't seem to be any Mad Max-style gangs wielding spiked clubs and chainsaws. Instead, the streets are filled with children returning from school, young mothers pushing battered prams, and old ladies pulling tartan shopping carts behind them. It's almost disappointing. Still, it makes it easier for her to push on through like a professional.

Sam clutches her bag and ventures up to the front door, careful to avoid the dog excrement that dots the path. She rings the doorbell and finds herself face to face with a woman who could honestly fall anywhere between twenty-five and fifty years old. The woman's dirty blonde hair doesn't look like it had been brushed or washed in weeks. The tiny baby clasped to her chest appears to have recently thrown up on her faded yellow t-shirt. Either she hasn't noticed, or she's just given up on hygiene.

Nevertheless, Sam extends her hand and introduces herself.

The woman takes her hand and shakes it. "I'm Mary. I'm sorry about the state of the place. It's hard enough to keep on top of things with my mum and the little ones to contend with. And ever since Daryl— Well . . . you know."

Sam shakes her head. "No need to apologise, Mary. I'm a single mum myself."

Mary gives her a sad smile and disappears inside without another word, leaving the door ajar. Sam follows her down a cramped hallway that smells of wet dog and stale tobacco, then into a small living room. The furniture is probably older than Sam, mismatched in colour, fabric and style. The carpet is stained and threadbare in places. In one of the chairs, an ancient woman festers, hazed in cigarette smoke. Mary sits on the sofa and pulls up her t-shirt so her baby can feed. Sam sits in the remaining chair and gathers her notes.

"So, first off I want to thank you for asking me here," she begins. "I know it's not easy going through the same details over and over again, so let's keep this fairly light. I'll ask for specifics where I need them, okay?" Mary nods, a little relieved. "So, can you tell me what happened to Daryl?"

Mary shifts position and pauses, weighing her words. "He went out with his mates, like he usually does on Friday night, and . . . he didn't come back. I wasn't too shocked, you know. Sometimes he sleeps over at Paul's house to save the taxi fare. Walks home in the morning. He says it's quite nice, really. I didn't think anything was wrong until . . . " Mary pauses, and a single tear runs down her cheek that she swiftly wipes away, "until the police called in the morning to say they'd found him in the canal."

Great, thinks Sam. *Another drunk.* She pulls what she hopes is a sympathetic smile and tries to work out how quickly she can conclude the interview without appearing rude. "What makes you think Daryl's death wasn't just a tragic accident? If he was out with his mates, couldn't it just be an accident? Drunken shenanigans gone wrong?"

Mary bristles at the comment. "Well, for one thing, he didn't drink. Didn't have the stomach for it. Give him a pint, and he'd likely chuck it up, so he never touched the stuff. He was sober as a judge when he died. No question."

"I understand, but—forgive me—how can you know that?"

"Because he was on the phone, wasn't he! Leaving a bleedin' voicemail when it happened."

The woman suddenly has Sam's full attention. "You have a recording of it? What did the police say about that?"

Mary gives Sam a sour smile. "Fucking plod deleted it 'accidentally', but I backed my phone up before I gave it to 'em. Fucking numpties. "

Sam leans forward, "Would you— I realise this is difficult but, Mary . . . would you mind if I listen to it?"

Grief cracks Mary's face, shattering the stoic façade she's been forced to adopt for the sake of her children. "No," she says, shaking her head. "I can't. I don't want to hear that again. It's too— I just . . . I can't."

Sam's heart sinks. This might be the first objective, concrete evidence that something dodgy is going on. The fact that the investigating officer deleted the original file is not lost on her either. However, she doesn't want to push the woman too hard, sensing that she'll be kicked out quick smart if she causes any upset here. Mary may have been forced to keep up appearances, but there has been a tension in the atmosphere since she brought up the drinking that Sam can't ignore. Sam nods and says, "I understand how painful that would feel for you, but this may contain information that can help prove what you and your group have been saying all along. Can you send me the file so I can listen to it later? It really could help."

"I can Bluetooth the file to you if you want?" says Mary.

Sam grins. "You'd be a lifesaver."

The two women spend the next ten minutes flicking through settings on their phones and swearing until the file transfer is complete. Once it's done, Mary asks, "You need anything else?"

"I think I've got everything I need for now. You've been very helpful. More than you know. I suppose one last thing I'd like to know is what you think happened to Daryl?"

The old woman, who has remained silent up to this point mutters, "Ginny got 'im. Useless fucker got too close to the water, and Ginny gobbled 'im up."

Mary turns to her mother and snaps, "Fucks sake, Ma, will you knock it off with that shite! Ginny Greenteeth's nowt but an old wives' tale to keep kiddies away from duck ponds."

The old woman cackles, delighting in the sharp reaction. "You say that now, girl, but I remember the stories growing up in the Pool. 'There is a lady on the mount; who she is, I do not know.' You damn well kept away from the water, 'cause Ginny Greenteeth would reach out from the duckweed with her spindly fingers and swallow you whole."

Sam feels an ice finger run down her spine. "Ginny Greenteeth? I've not heard this one."

The young woman's face can barely contain her disgust. "Nothing for you to worry about, luv. Just an old Liverpool folk story that mam won't shut up about and I've had enough of listening to." She turns back to her mother and says, "You hear me, Ma? Even if your Ginny Greenteeth was real, what the fuck would she be doing in the Manchester Shipping Canal, eh? Liverpool's forty fucking miles away. What did she do? Get on a fucking bus? Give it a rest!"

The argument between mother and daughter intensifies after that. When the baby adds its cries to the cacophony, Sam slips out the front door, thanking Mary for her time.

The streets are quieter now, and gangs of youths have begun to congregate. A stab of discomfort hurries her steps.

She starts the car and is about to pull away when she notices a missed call on her phone, an answerphone message flashing. Without checking the number on the missed call, she opens the message, hoping that Sarah has finally found some better accommodation. But instead, Chris Buchanan's voice crackles through the phone's speaker.

"Sam . . . It's Chris . . . Chris Buchanan. I need to see you. I've found something."

Sam takes a sip of her coffee and watches the entrance to the cafe with somewhat mixed feelings. It is fair to say that she has some pretty significant doubts about Chris Buchanan. He'd been barely lucid when she saw him last, and she can't help but wonder what state he will be in now, assuming he turns up at all. He seemed manic on the phone, barely coherent, clearly angry about something. Part of her hopes that he won't show. She's strung out and anxious from all the coffee and feels pretty rank in general. There is a faint tang of body odour creeping through her deodorant, her feet are sweaty inside her shoes, and she feels like she hasn't showered in a couple of days.

She retrieves her air-pods from her bag and scrolls through her phone until she comes to the audio file Mary sent across. *Might as well keep busy until Chris gets here*, she thinks. And if he hasn't arrived by the time she finishes her coffee, she'll block his number and get back to the farm. Last thing she needed now was to become the focus of some drunkard's hard-on.

A man's voice crackles through her headphones. Mary's missing husband. Sam isn't sure what she'd been expecting to hear, but the softly spoken Mancunian accent in her ears isn't it.

"Alright, love," Daryl says. "I'm heading home now. It was getting a bit messy down there. Billy was gonna chuck his guts up or start a fight, and I didn't fancy cleaning either of them up. I'll be about twenty minutes. Half hour tops. I'll crash on the sofa if you're in bed, so I don't wake you and the baby up. Love you."

Sam has to admit that there isn't any trace of a slur in Daryl's voice. He sounds normal. Sober and actually pretty nice as it goes.

"Hang on, love . . . I think there's someone . . . Hello? Is there someone there? Are you alright? Oh god! SOMEONE HELP ME! PLEASE!"

The recording cuts off with a scream that sounds too high, too shrill for a man. Sam rips the earpieces out and stares at her phone as if it's turned into a fat spider in her hand. She reaches for her coffee cup with trembling fingers and almost screams herself as another hand reaches across to touch hers.

"Jesus, Sam. Are you OK?" asks Chris, sliding into the seat opposite her.

She looks up at him, heart racing. "Yeah . . . sure . . . Sorry, I'm just— You surprised me, is all."

Chris frowns. "Well, I don't think I've had a reaction from a woman like that since my ex-wife. Are you sure you're alright? You seem pretty shaken up."

"Well, don't creep up on people when they've got headphones in, then!" she snaps. "Listen, I've had a bastard of a day, and all I want to do is go home, soak in the shower and then go to bed. Don't piss about. You said you had something for me?"

His face wears an expression that might best be described as guilty puppy. "Well, first off, I'm sorry for startling you. It wasn't intentional. But yeah, I've been thinking about what you said yesterday, and I started doing some digging of my own."

He opens his backpack and retrieves a battered laptop that might have been considered state of the art when Sam was in school. "This will take a minute or two to start up, so bear with me," he says while the elderly machine's hard drive whines and rattles.

Sam realises that Chris seems sober and more or less together. He's showered, shaved and changed his clothes at least. His eyes are still red-rimmed, and the bags under them could carry a weekly shop, but he actually appears lucid and focused. Wonders never cease.

He rattles something out on the keyboard, then meets Sam's eyes. "After you left, I tried to access the notes from my last case, but I was locked out of the detail. The whole file is restricted. At first, I thought they'd suspended my access to the case management system, so I looked at another file, which was fine."

Sam leans forward in her seat, suddenly interested. "And?"

"So, I looked at the file for that other case you mentioned, and I got the same thing. Restricted access. Which is bizarre because if I can access one file, I should be able to see literally anything in the system. They don't restrict these things on a case-by-case basis. You'll get in a world of trouble if you're caught snooping at things you aren't supposed to, but you should be able to access anything in theory once you are in. We need to be able to do that to link related cases."

"Oh. Is that all?" Sam says. "We'd already worked out that they were covering these things up. I don't see how this helps apart to confirm that something weird is going on."

Chris grins at her. It is the first time Sam has seen him smile. "I've not gotten to the best bit yet. I went back through all of the drownings in the North West for the last ten years—and there have been plenty of them as you might expect—but every once in a while I'd come across a restricted record. I'd get the location of the incident, date and name of the deceased, but everything else was restricted. So, when I started marking these on a map . . . well, see for yourself."

He turns the laptop around and shows Sam the screen. It is a map of the North West of England, going as far south as Liverpool, then North to Preston.

"Jesus!" says Sam. "That looks like—"

"A pattern," Chris says. "Yeah. It looks like it repeats every twenty-five years. It goes down as far as Liverpool, then stops for ten years before starting North again. I've not finished going back through all the data yet, but these incidents are twenty-five years apart in the same places, on the same date by the looks of things."

Sam can't take her eyes away from the laptop screen. If Chris is right, then this has been covered up for decades. Longer, perhaps. Her mind is spinning, spinning, and then she grasps what Chris is getting at. What should have been obvious to her immediately. "Fuck. So we know where it's going to strike next?"

"Two days from now, here," he says, jabbing his finger at the screen. "Barnfold Reservoir."

Sam feels absolutely exhausted by the time she reaches the farm track. Her mind is thick with fatigue. She hasn't the concentration to dwell on anything for long; the events of the day and the possible implications of them swirl through her thoughts like leaves caught in the wind.

Marcus is sitting on a bench beneath an old sycamore tree when she pulls up to the house. He raises his hand in greeting.

"Evenin', stranger," he calls as she gets out of the car. "There's still some food in the pot if you're hungry."

"Thanks, Marcus. I'll see how I feel after I have a shower. It's been a really long day."

"Take your time. We got connected to the water main about five years back, so it'll be nice and hot! No need to worry about running the well dry, either. I'll maybe see you when you've freshened up."

Sam feels a smile spread across her face. "Mains water? Wow, the old place really has joined the twenty-first century. You have no idea what I would have given for that when I was a teenager."

Marcus chuckles. "I suppose I might have been a bit rough on you over your long showers."

Sam feigns shock and says, "Long showers? Long? If I was in there for more than five minutes, you were banging on the door, reminding me about the well water."

"I reckon I was. I never understood why you needed to spend so long in there, though."

"I have *hair*, unlike some people," she says with a wink. "And it was a lot longer when I was a teenager, do you remember? It took ages to get the conditioner out of it. There were times I needed to go and finish rinsing it with a bucket of cold water."

Marcus laughed at that. "Well, you can take your time tonight. Wash your hair as much as you like."

"Thanks, Marcus. Really. You've been a life saver. I'll see you in a little while."

Sam retrieves her bag from the car and goes through the front door. Both children are in the living room. Julia is colouring a picture of a dog while George is watching a movie on the TV.

"Hi guys," she says. "Have you had a nice time?"

Julia carefully clicks the lid on, then puts her felt-tip down on the sofa and runs over, throwing her arms around Sam. "We've had such a nice day. We went for a long walk with Grandad Marcus, and I got to feed some baby cows with one of his friends. They're so cuuuuute!"

Sam returns the hug and says, "That's lovely, sweetheart." A sudden shriek from the TV makes her jump and she looks up in time to see a machete plunge into the skull of a scantily clad blonde. "George, what on earth are you watching?"

"Nothing," he replies, eyes locked to the screen.

"It doesn't look like nothing to me," she snaps, and picks up the remote control. She pauses the movie and confirms the age rating. "George, you can't watch things like this. You're far too young! It'll give you nightmares."

George gets to his feet, snatches up the iPad and yells at her. "You never let me do anything! It's not fair!" Then he storms out of the room and up the stairs, each footfall sounding like a twenty-stone rugby player. His door slams hard enough that Sam feels the vibration through the floor.

"What the hell?" she mutters, a little shocked at the outburst.

"Don't worry, mummy," says Julia, loyal to the last. "He's been in a bad mood all day."

Sam smiles tightly and pats her shoulder. "Thank you. I'll have a word with him later. I— I think I'm going to have a shower now. I'll see you when I get out."

Sam spends longer in the shower than she intends. On some level, she's doing it for her teenage self as an act of retrospective rebellion, but mainly she just enjoys the feel of the hot water pummelling her skin, washing her tension away. Still, she feels a stab of apprehension when she finishes and it's time to go back downstairs. The last thing she wants is another row with George. These days she doesn't seem to be able to say anything to the boy without setting him off, and it's starting to wear on her nerves. She can't just let him get away with it, can she? *Damn.* She resolves to have a talk with him tomorrow about both his viewing choices and a little thing called self-control. Perhaps Marcus can help her figure out how to broach the subject.

She walks down the stairs to find a hot plate of pasta and a large glass of white wine waiting for her on the table. Marcus waits at the table, reading a book about cyber-security of all things. He looks up smiling.

"Thank you, Marcus. This looks amazing. You needn't have gone to the trouble."

"It's no bother, lass. I put your wine in the freezer to cool it down while you were in the shower, and I dished up when the pipes stopped groaning."

She sits and takes a sip, relishing the cold, clean taste of the wine. "Well, it's greatly appreciated—and not just the food. All of it. You've been an absolute godsend these past few days. I don't know what I would have done without you."

"Don't think anything of it, love. Truth be told, I've enjoyed having you here more than I can say. I've managed well enough over the years, but the old place has been pretty quiet for a long time now. It's doing my heart good to have a bit of light and laughter in here again."

"Marcus, I— I'm sorry that I lost touch with you. Deeply. I don't really have any excuse. I think it was hard for me after mum died, and then . . . and then once I went to university, life just seemed to move so fast."

"You don't have to apologise, love. I know what it can be like. And, as I said, I've come to realise that I should have been a better parent to you. I didn't want you to think I was trying to replace your mam, so I kept my distance, like. Gave you your space. Too much space, I dare say. I'm sorry for that. I hope I can make up for it in some small way now, with you and your little ones."

Sam smiles. "You've more than made up for it. And you'll see a lot more of us in future, I promise. I want to do something for you, to thank you properly. Will you let me take you out for dinner somewhere nice next week?"

"You don't need to, love. You don't owe me anything."

"I want to. Please let me."

Sam can't make out the expression on her uncle's face at first, then it dawns on her: he's crying. She reaches across the table, taking his hand in hers. "Are you alright?"

He squeezes her hand and then wipes his eyes. "Don't worry about me. I'm just being a daft old bugger. Aye, that would be lovely, lass. If you're sure."

"I'm completely sure. Is there anywhere you'd like to go?"

"I'll have a think about it and let you know. Thank you, love. Now, I'm going to leave you to it and get an early night. I'm taking the kids out for the day, and we'll be up at the crack of dawn."

A thought occurs to Sam and she acts on impulse. "Are you up for some company? I've got to be up early on Sunday morning, but I can move some of my other appointments around—spend the day with you and the kids for a change. If that doesn't mess up your plans too much?"

Marcus's eyes widen a little at her suggestion. "No, love. That would be wonderful," he croaks. "Are you sure your boss won't mind?"

"Naah. Bollocks to him. It's Saturday and I've earned a day off. Anyway, it's been a long time since we've spent any real time together, and it'd be lovely to actually go out somewhere with the kids for a change. I can't remember the last time we did anything special together."

"Then it's settled," Marcus says and rises from the table, just as a scream rings out from the rear of the property.

Sam's heart lurches and she looks wide-eyed at her uncle. "Marcus—where are the kids?"

The old man's expression of shock and concern mirrors her own. "They went to bed . . . I mean, they *said* . . . "

Sam is out of the chair before her uncle is able to finish the sentence, her glass of wine shattering on the quarry tiled floor. She throws open the back door to the farmhouse and races outside as the screams intensify.

Sam feels her legs turn to rubber as she takes in the scene. George is standing by the edge of Miller's Pond while Julia is in the water up to her waist. She tries to get out, but every time she scrambles to the shore, George shoves her back in with a laugh."

"GEORGE!" she yells, "What the *fuck* are you doing? Let her out this *instant!*"

George turns to face her, his face flushed. "What?" he stammers, "I wasn't doing anything!"

Sam reaches the twins just as Julia manages to clamber from the water, her clothes dripping wet. Her relief at seeing her daughter out of the pond is fleeting when she sees the devious smirk on her son's face. "Wasn't doing anything? I'll fucking show you what nothing is, you little shit!" she screams, as her hand raises almost of its own accord. Before it can descend, however, she feels a strong hand grasp her wrist, holding it fast.

"Julia, go inside and get out of those wet clothes," says Marcus in a calm but firm voice. "George, I think you should go inside and go straight to bed. We'll talk more in the morning."

"But it's not my fault," George begins to protest, but then seems to think better of arguing his case and vanishes after his sister into the house.

Marcus releases Sam's arm and says, "Best take a breath, love.

You don't want to be doing anything you'll regret come the morning."

Sam almost collapses to the floor, the adrenaline still coursing through her veins. "I . . . I can't believe he did that . . . I can't believe *I* almost hit him . . . I've never raised a hand to either of them before, Marcus. But just seeing Julia in that fucking pond and George finding it so fucking funny . . . I just . . . "

Marcus put a hand on Sam's shoulder. "I know, love. We all do things in the heat of the moment, and with what happened to your mum . . . It's understandable. Why don't you go inside and have another glass of your wine to calm down a bit."

Sam nods and starts walking away from the pond when she realises that Marcus isn't following her. "Aren't you coming?"

"No, love," he says. "I'm going to do what I should have done the moment you all arrived. I'm going to board that damn pond up."

CHAPTER SIX

"**WAKE UP, MUMMY!**" Julia yells and leaps onto Sam's single bed.

Her mind still caught between the weeds and the waking world, Sam somehow manages to stop herself lashing out at her daughter. She'd been fighting something in her dreams. Fighting for her life. Now she's fighting for breath, the air driven from her lungs by Julia's sharp knees.

"Julia," she gasps, cracking open one eye, then the next. "What time is it? Is something the matter?"

Julia begins bouncing up and down. "It's almost six, lazybones," she laughs. "Grandad Marcus, George and me have been up for ages, so it's time for you to get up, too."

Sam pulls the duvet back over her head. "It's too early, love. You go watch TV or something. I'll be down in a couple of hours."

The duvet disappears from Sam's body, dragged down in a single movement like a magician whipping a tablecloth out from beneath a bone china tea set. "No, mummy, you have to get up now. We're all going out for the day, remember?"

Sam groans as the memory comes back to her. She'd told Marcus she'd join them for the day last night before she went to bed. It seemed like a good idea at the time. It had been ages since she'd had a proper day out with the kids. When was that? she wonders. *Chessington maybe? Christ, that must have been two years ago.* She feels ashamed that she's not done more with the children, but she's always been so busy. Plus, if she remembers correctly, that day out at the theme park had cost her well over two hundred pounds, which was not an inconsiderable sum of money on her salary. She groans, "Okay, okay, I'm coming. Go back downstairs. I'll be there in a minute."

Julia bounds off the bed, skips to the door, then turns to face

73

her mother. "Don't you go sneaking back to sleep now, mum. Like you do on a Saturday when you've been drinking."

A fresh wave of shame washes over Sam. *Am I really that bad? Am I hungover that often?* Yes, she realises. She is. A few drinks with Heidi after work or, if she's out of town, just a bottle of red in front of the TV. It was a regular Friday night event . . . . that had turned into a few drinks on Saturday to chase away the last lingering shreds of her hangover—plus a few drinks on Sunday of course, to drag the weekend out as long as she could. It had become habitual without her even realising it, or at least without admitting it to herself. "I'm not hungover, sweetie. I didn't have anything to drink last night."

Julia raises her right eyebrow, suddenly looking far older than her years, and she even puts her hands on her hips. In other circumstances it might have been funny. "Where did that bottle of wine come from then? Did the wine fairies leave it on the kitchen table to get you into trouble?"

Sam swings her legs off the bed and stands up. "There you go. I'm up now," she says, a little irritated. "I'll be down as soon as I've had a wash and cleaned my teeth. Is that alright with you, your majesty?"

Julia seems satisfied and skips out the door, calling "Love you, mummy!" over her shoulder.

Sam trudges around her bed and opens the curtains, filling the room with weak light. It is always like this at the farm. Even after the sun rises, it takes an age to clear the hills properly and for the first golden fingers of light to drive away the lingering shadows. She glances down at Miller's Pond and finds that Marcus has been as good as his word. Instead of the duckweed covered surface, the pond has been covered by heavy railway sleepers, bolted together in a rough frame. The relief she feels is palpable. As if the monster that haunted her nightmares had a stake driven through its heart and buried. Grabbing a pile of fresh clothes, Sam stumbles to the bathroom to get herself ready.

She walks downstairs fifteen minutes later, feeling at least vaguely human, if not entirely wide awake. She smells freshly brewed coffee mingling with the delicious aroma of frying bacon, and her stomach growls appreciation. Marcus and the kids sit at the old farmhouse table with their plates piled high with sausages, bacon, fried eggs, mushrooms, baked beans and hash browns.

Marcus nurses a mug of coffee while the children have juice boxes standing by.

"Morning all," she says, attempting brightness. "Hope you left some of that food for me. It smells delicious."

Marcus smiles at her. "Morning, sleepyhead. There's a plate keeping warm in the stove, and the coffee's in the pot. Help yourself."

Sam retrieves her food then pours herself a large mug of coffee before sitting down. "Morning, George. I'm sorry about our argument last night, but what you were doing was very dangerous and I got scared. Can we put it behind us?"

George twists his torso ninety degrees to look at the wall, then puts his hand up to his face to block his mother from his peripheral vision.

"George!" Sam says, a little shocked and hurt. "That's very rude. Can you answer me when I talk to you, please?"

George shrugs but keeps his hand in place, refusing to look at his mother. Julia puts her hand on Sam's arm and says, "I think he's still cross about last night, mummy. Please don't start a fight with him, or it'll spoil our day."

Sam weighs this up and decides not to push the matter. At least, not yet. She's also conscious that her daughter has been the more adult of the two of them in the house this morning.

"Fine," she sighs. "So, Marcus, what's the plan for the day?"

Her uncle smiles at her. "That would be telling, now, wouldn't it?" The older man winks at Julia, who begins to giggle. Even George seems to be smirking from behind his hands. "Am I missing something?" she asks.

Julia lets out a snort of laughter at this, and George is visibly shaking behind his hand, although he's still not prepared to look his mother in the face. Sam suddenly senses that she is on the outside of the family unit, looking in, and it's a feeling she doesn't like—not one little bit.

She gives Marcus a quizzical look and he says, "Nothing to worry about, love. Young Julia was doing an impression of you yesterday, and she was pretty spot on."

Julia lightly slaps Marcus's arm, squealing, "Grandad! You weren't supposed to tell on me! You are such a snitch!"

Marcus grins back at Julia. "Guilty as charged. Now, go and wash your plates up. We aren't going anywhere until all these breakfast dishes are all put away."

To Sam's shock, Julia collects all the crockery up, fills the sink and begins washing up. To compound her astonishment, George then picks up a tea towel and starts drying the clean plates before putting them away in the cupboard.

"OK," she says to Marcus, "who are these two imposters and what have you done with my real children?"

"They've been as good as gold since they've been here. You've done a grand job with 'em. Why? Do they not help out at home?"

"No!" Sam says with some asperity. "They don't. If I even suggest it, they act like I'd asked them to eat broken glass. I don't know what you're doing to them, but by all means, keep doing it."

Marcus gives Sam a small salute, "Aye, skipper," he says, then leans over to the children. "Right, you two. Get your things together. We're leaving in five minutes."

Julia and George need no further encouragement and dash to the front door, putting their shoes on enthusiastically.

Sam takes a last mouthful of her breakfast and gives Marcus her compliments. "So, spill the beans, then. Where are we going?"

"Ah," Marcus says, giving her an enigmatic smile, "I wouldn't want to spoil the surprise."

"Are we there yet?"

Marcus turns to look at Julia and says, "Not long now, darling. If you keep an eye out, you might start to get some clues as to where we're going."

Julia begins bouncing up and down in the rear seat of the elderly truck and calls out the name on every sign to see if that's their destination. To each one, Marcus grins and gives the same reply. "Nope."

Sam cranes her neck to see George looking at her iPad. She can't stop herself from commenting. "George," she says, "If you keep looking at the iPad while we're driving, you might get car sick. Would you like to play eye-spy with me instead?"

"I'm fine," George says, fingers flicking the screen.

Sam shakes her head and wonders if it's possible for puberty to start at eight years old.

"I'll play with you, mummy," chirps Julia, giving up her attempts to guess their destination.

Sam smiles, grateful for her happy, cheerful daughter. The two twins couldn't be more different. George had always existed more inside his head, subject to dark moods, much like Sam herself. Julia was much more like Brian had been. She is so energetic and enthusiastic and doesn't have a thought enter her mind that she doesn't verbalise. She loves both her children, but Julia is definitely the easier of the pair to deal with, apart from her night terrors.

"OK," she says. "I spy, with my little eye, something beginning with . . . Z!"

Julia's brow furrows, and she begins looking around. "Oh, mummy. You picked a really hard one to start with," she says. Then the girl notices the brown sign coming up with an elephant on it. "Is it a zoo? Are we going to the zoo? Oh my god!" she yells and begins bouncing up and down on the back seat with enough force to rock the suspension.

"Aye, lass. Well guessed. We're going to the Cumbria Safari Zoo. I bought the tickets online yesterday."

Sam shakes her head in appreciation. "Oh, Marcus, you shouldn't have. That must have cost a fortune."

"Don't you worry about that. The way I see it, I've got a fair few birthdays and Christmases to make up for. Besides," he says, winking at her, "I found some vouchers online. The little uns get in free with two adult tickets. That means there's some cash left over so they can feed the animals, too."

Julia almost ends up in the front seat when she hears this. "We get to feed them? OH MY GOD! Which animals, Grandad Marcus? Can I feed the monkeys? And the giraffes? And the red pandas?"

The old man lets out a hearty chuckle. "We'll find out when we get there, love. Now, settle down a bit, or you'll bounce my old truck right off the road."

Julia sits in her seat with a massive grin on her face, wringing her hands in excitement. Sam can't remember the last time she saw her daughter looking so happy, and she promises herself then and there that she'll make time to do more with the children. They are growing so fast, and time is just slipping away. Seeing Julia's unbridled joy sends a rush of warmth through Sam's chest. Even George has broken into a smile despite himself, though when he realises Sam has noticed, the smile disappears once more.

After another few minutes, they arrive at the zoo, and Marcus parks his pickup truck beneath the shade of a large sycamore tree. Julia is out of the car almost before the vehicle stops moving.

"Julia, don't run off—and watch out for traffic!" Sam shouts to the girl, who is already making a beeline for the entrance. Julia waves to her mother, completely ignores her instructions and almost sprints to the gate. Sam shakes her head and admits defeat. Animals are Julia's favourite things in the world, and the trip Marcus has arranged is as close to heaven for the girl as possible. She starts following her daughter, then notices George lagging behind, his head down, hands stuffed into his pockets.

"Marcus," she says, "can you catch up with Julia and keep an eye on her, please? I need to have a quick word with George."

Marcus nods then trots across the car park to Julia. Sam walks over to her son and asks what is wrong.

"Nothing," he mutters without looking up.

"It's not nothing. Are you still angry because of last night? Or is there something else because, honestly, I don't know what I've done wrong. I'm getting pretty sick of this. Marcus has spent a lot of money for you here, and you'll end up spoiling it for everyone if you don't snap out of this mood."

The boy raises his head and looks Sam in the eyes for the first time in days. His glare is white hot. "It's you! You always leave. Again and again. You leave us with Grandma Janet, then you leave us with Grandad Marcus, or you go out with Auntie Heidi and leave us with the babysitter. You hate us! You don't want to be around us, and now you're leaving us again."

"Oh, George. I'm right here. And I'm sorry that I'm so busy, but you understand I *have* to work, right? To earn money so we can have nice things. If your dad were still around, I wouldn't have to work so hard, and I could spend more time with you, but that's not how things worked out."

George pulls his hand from hers, "All of our things are rubbish, and I don't want things anyway. I want my mum!"

Sam wraps her arms around her son, "Oh, sweetheart, I'm sorry. I'm so sorry. I know I've not been there for you much lately, but I'm here now, so we can have a nice day together. And I'll try to be better in future, I promise."

George pulls away from her. "Liar! You're going away again tomorrow."

Sam struggles to keep her voice from breaking when she

replies. "I know, George. I have to go somewhere tomorrow, but I don't have any choice. I promise you this, though—when I finish this job, I'll take some time off and we can spend some proper time together again before you go back to school. I just— I can't do anything about tomorrow."

George turns his back on her, mutters something acidic then hurries after the others.

Sam joins them once she's dried her tears and pulled herself together. Despite it being early on a Saturday morning, the zoo is not particularly busy, with only a few other families and small groups ahead of them. Julia sprints to a large map, beside herself with excitement, and she squeals at the scale of the place.

"Oh, can we see the pandas first? I love the red pandas! Or the monkeys? No! The giraffes!"

Marcus puts his hand on her shoulder and smiles at the girl. "We've got all day, darling, but look, here's the schedule. We're going to the penguins first. Then it's the giraffes, lemurs, bears, and the red pandas. You can feed them all if you want. How's that, eh?"

Julia examines the map, locating the penguin enclosure, then she grabs her brother's hand and practically drags him down the path.

Marcus turns to Sam and says, "Is everything alright, love? I saw you and young George have a bit of a set to in the car park, and you looked upset."

Sam sighs. "He's angry because I'm never around. He says I always leave him, and he's right. He's right! I try my best, Marcus, but it's so hard doing this on my own. Sometimes, I wonder if I'd be better off living on benefits and taking care of them properly rather than killing myself doing this bloody job. It's not like my wages are that much better. I don't want them growing up, resenting me the way I—"

She covers her mouth, horrified by the words that were about to emerge. Marcus takes Sam's hand and pulls it away gently. She looks at him, pained, ridden with guilt and shame. Demonstrations of affection from her uncle are alien to her.

"It's alright, love. You can say it. I know well enough. The way you resented me."

Sam squeezes her uncle's hand." I'm sorry, but it's true. This is so messed up. I see how you are with them, and then I remember how you were with me and . . . I guess I just wish things had been different." She gives him a sad smile. "As strange as it seems, I've been jealous."

"I'm sorry, love. I truly am. The loss of your mother hit me hard. Harder than I expected. For a long time, I didn't know how I was going to carry on. I shut myself off from you because I was scared of getting too close. I just didn't think I could go through it again, so I kept my distance. I tried to do right by you, but I was so caught up in my grief that I never considered what it was doing to you. You needed more from me than food on the table or a roof over your head. That's what my therapist said, anyhow, and I see it. I want to be better."

Sam raises an eyebrow. "You have a therapist? I never thought you'd be the type. You've been full of surprises these past few days."

Marcus chuckles. "Aye, I wouldn't have thought about it either. Didn't seem to be much point raking over the past. My mate Graham saw what it was doing to me, though, and he put me in touch with someone he knows. Good man, that Graham. It took a while for me to come to terms with things, but I got there in the end. I just— Sam, I just hope you can find it in your heart to forgive me."

Sam pulls her uncle into a tight embrace before he notices her eyes welling up. She's not ready to cry in front of him yet. "It's OK. I understand. I really do. And you were right in a way. There's no point dwelling on the past. We can't do anything about it; all we can do is make sure we don't keep making the same stupid mistakes. Oh, Marcus, what am I going to do? George has so much anger in him, but I don't know what I can do about it. I'm doing to him all the same stupid things I was angry at you for."

"You're a good mum, love. Don't you ever forget that. And one day, he'll see the sacrifices you've made for him and his sister. He's young, and he doesn't understand. Give him time, and he'll come to accept the bigger picture."

Sam gives her uncle another tight squeeze, then releases him. "Thanks, Marcus. I hope you're right, I really do."

"I know I am, love. Don't you worry. I'll have a word with him later and explain things to him. Now, we'd better catch up to the young 'uns, or we'll miss the penguins."

Sam smiles and walks down the gravel path after her children. She feels that a weight has been lifted, though not entirely removed.

The show is about to start when they arrive at the penguin enclosure. An array of smart-looking birds line up while the zookeeper walks up and down, telling the assembled families about the various names and personalities.

"You're just in time. The show is about to start!" As Sam takes the chair beside her, Julia's nose wrinkles, and she whispers, "Mummy? Are they supposed to smell that bad?"

Sam is exhausted by the time they return to the truck and begin the journey back to the farm. She honestly can't remember enjoying herself so much for a long time. Even George snapped out of his mood when he got the chance to feed a leopard with a large chunk of meat attached to a long metal pole. He never looked so thrilled in his life. The junk food, fizzy drinks and ice cream kept both children hyperactive and buzzing as they'd flitted from show to show. Sam had thought that Julia might try to smuggle one of the red pandas into her bag, and watched her like a hawk, but she settled for an overpriced stuffed toy panda instead. Both children were now fast asleep on the back seat of Marcus's truck, while the two adults sat in comfortable silence, listening to oldies on the radio.

They began the final leg of the journey, wending down familiar roads. The sense of nostalgia is comforting now, rather than the disorientation she felt a few days before. Finally, she turns to Marcus and says, "I've been thinking about what you said earlier. I was wondering how you'd feel if the kids and I relocated a bit closer? It's just a thought at the moment, but I think it might be good for me to move away from the city. If I took a less demanding job up here, I could spend more time with the kids, and you could spend more time with them as well. And with me."

Moisture seems to accumulate in the corner of the old man's eyes, filling the cracks and wrinkles with silver trails. "Love, there's nothing that would make me happier. Truly. I know nowt's set in stone just yet, but if that's what you think is best, there will always be a home for you here. For you all."

Sam squeezes his hand. "Thank you, Marcus. It means more than you know. As I say, it's just a thought for now, and there would be an awful lot to sort out with schools and such. And something more permanent would need to be done about that fucking pond. But if we could live here, it might solve a lot of problems."

The truck rumbles over the cattle grid and along the winding track that leads to the farm. As they approach the main farmhouse, Marcus's shoulders stiffen. There's a brand-new Audi parked by the rear door.

"That's odd. Were you expecting visitors?"

Marcus shakes his head. "No. You?"

"I can't see why anyone would come here looking for me. No one really knows I'm here, and no one at work could afford a car that nice."

The truck pulls into its usual spot, and then Marcus and Sam get out, leaving the children asleep in the back seat. As they begin walking towards the car, the door opens and a tall, blonde, elegantly dressed woman gets out.

"Heidi! What on earth are you doing here?"

"Do I need to have a reason to come visit my bestie?" Heidi asks, stepping gingerly through the muck. She embraces Sam and kisses her on both cheeks, then she holds out her hand to Marcus. "Hi, you must be the uncle. I'm Heidi. I'm sure Sam's told you all about me. Thank you for taking care of her in her hour of need."

The truck's rear door flies open, and the children practically hurl themselves at the woman. "Auntie Heidi!" Julia squeals, hugging her fiercely.

Sam grins at her friend, but she's a little nonplussed. "It's amazing to see you, H, but you still haven't told me what the hell you're doing here?"

Heidi waves it away. "When you told me what happened with that disgusting hotel, I decided to switch assignments. I'm doing a piece on some new fashion house in Manchester now, so I could help you out of this mess. I got the magazine to pay for a suite in the Hilton for the next two weeks. There's plenty of space for you and the kids to share with me, and we can live it up properly. You deserve a holiday. I'm going to be mostly doing the interviews in the evening, so the little monsters and I can see the sights while you finish your piece. Won't that be nice! You can relax in the lap of luxury instead of imposing on your dear old uncle here."

Sam shakes her head, "I don't know what to say, H. You didn't have to do that. And we're doing fine here. Really."

"I know you can rough it with the best of them, darling, but it's awfully . . . rural, isn't it. And you don't have to suffer. Auntie Heidi to the rescue! I'll let you get the first round in to thank me."

"First round? What?"

Heidi winks at Sam, "Well, as long as your lovely uncle is happy taking care of the sprogs for one more night, I figure you can show me the sights of your hometown. So come on! Get your glad rags on. We're long overdue a girls' night out."

CHAPTER SEVEN

"**HONEY, WE HAVE ARRIVED!**" Heidi exclaims, flinging open the bar's double doors.

Sam shuffles after her, feeling somewhat self-conscious. Heidi is dressed to kill, as ever. She wears a form-fitting dress with a floral print accentuating every curve. If anyone can take their eyes off that, they'll see a pair of Jimmy Choos on her feet, and an Armani handbag which probably cost more than Sam's monthly salary. By contrast, Sam is wearing one of her nicer work blouses and a knee-length skirt, with work shoes that have frankly seen better days. She shouldn't be surprised, she tells herself. This is how it's always been. She has accepted her role as the plainer, less flamboyant friend who tends to fade into the background. However, the last thing Sam expected to do was go out for a night on the town when she packed for the trip, and her unpreparedness only accentuates the differences. Heidi offered to loan her one of her outfits, but, given the difference in their shapes and heights, Sam was pretty sure she'd look like someone had wrapped a water-filled balloon in cling film, so she'd politely declined.

Heidi grabs a table close to the dance floor and waves over a server, ordering for them both. Heidi loves to party, and this gives Sam pause. Her friend's modus-operandi is to get her alcohol levels up as quickly as possible, then let loose.

The bar is a neon and chrome assault on the senses. The dancefloor looks like a mirror ball, with a mosaic of reflective pieces beneath what seems to be tempered glass. Whenever the overhead laser lights sweep across it, the beams bounce off in all different directions. The walls are mostly mirrored too, with neon signs and chrome shelving running the length of the place. It's pretty intense. Toward the front of the bar is a seating area where they are still serving food to some of the more conservatively dressed diners while the party crowd filter through for their night's drinking and dancing. Sam is painfully aware that she and Heidi are at least a decade older than the other dancers, but Heidi is oblivious. The music is pure Magaluf, with a bass line that thumps through the bones.

"What did you order us?" Sam yells over the music.

"Two-for-one cocktails, baby! We've got a mojito and a blue lagoon each, plus two jägerbombs to start us off."

Sam groans. "You know I can't have a late one, right? I'm meeting someone for work at seven tomorrow morning. I can't do that dying on my arse."

Heidi pouts. "You're no fun anymore. But I promise to be good. Don't worry, Cinderella; I'll have you home by midnight."

Sam doesn't believe a word of it but promises herself that she'll be in a taxi well before that, no matter how much Heidi whines and pleads.

Their drinks arrive, and Heidi raises her jägerbomb. "Here's to getting you the fuck out of that farm and away from your creepy-ass uncle."

She downs the drink in one and turns the glass over on the table. Sam throws her own drink back, then takes a sip of her mojito to get rid of the taste. No one drinks jägerbombs for pleasure, she reminds herself. They have a specific purpose. At least the energy drink element should wake her up. She's still pretty exhausted after the day at the zoo.

"Actually," she says, wagging a finger, "Marcus has been great these last few days. The kids love him, and the two of us have sorted a lot of stuff out."

"Really? Ever since I've known you, all you've done is tell me what a fucking arsehole he is. 'A cold, distant, uncaring, miserable fuck' was the phrase, I believe."

Sam shrugs. "What can I say? It's been a long time, and he's changed a lot. He saw a therapist and everything. "

"Na, fuck that noise. Did you see the look he gave me when I got out of the car? He wanted to take an axe to me."

"In fairness, love, you were a bit of a cow to him. 'Somewhere less . . . rural,' I think you said?"

Heidi drains half of her Blue Lagoon and grins. "Well, it's hardly Texworld Evolution Paris, is it? More like Texas Chainsaw Massacre!"

"Apart from it being in Lancashire instead of Texas?"

"OK, I'll concede that point. But I ask you this. Does Marcus have a chainsaw?"

Sam lets out a snort of laughter. "Yeah. A big one. He uses it to chop up firewood then sells it. He drives truckloads of logs round to neighbouring farms for their log burners."

"There you go!" Heidi says with a triumphant expression plastered across her face. "I rest my case. The sooner we get you and the sprogs back to civilisation, the better."

Sam takes a large gulp of her mojito, feeling the ice cubes clink against her teeth. She isn't looking forward to the next part of the conversation. "Well, I don't know if I want to, H. Not yet, at least. The kids are having a great time, and Marcus seems to be having a real impact on them. They listen to him. Christ, they've even started washing the breakfast dishes. And it's doing them a world of good to get out in the fresh air. And to meet a grandparent that's a bit less . . . Janet."

A hurt expression flickers across Heidi's face, just for a second before the mask is back in place once more. "Fair enough, I suppose. Not sure swapping Annie Wilkes for Leatherface is the best choice, but I get that you want your choice of poor adult role models to be well rounded."

"Seriously, he's not that bad. The opposite, in fact. He's been brilliant." Sam pauses, worried about how her friend will react to the next part of the conversation. "So much so that I'm thinking of staying on up here after I finish the assignment. A fresh start, you know."

Heidi puts her drink down and frowns. "A fresh start? You're not on about a holiday, are you? You're actually thinking about moving here! Why the fuck would you want to do something like that?"

"You don't know how hard it has been for me, Heidi, these last few years."

"What the hell do you mean by that? Who else sits with you night after night, listening to you vent about your shitty job and what a bitch Janet is, and how your gorgeous little kids are massive shitbags really, if only I knew, hey? Who dropped everything to be with you when Brian—"

Heidi bites back on the last bit, embarrassed by her outburst. She knocks back the rest of her Lagoon. Sam reaches across the table and takes her friend's hand. "That's not what I mean. And I appreciate all you've done for me, truly. But H, I can barely afford the flat on my salary as it is. Think what it'll be like in a year or two when the kids start needing separate rooms. I'm gonna need a three-bedroom place and London is just too fucking expensive. I've been working all the hours god sends just to keep my head above water, and I'm missing their childhood. I can't keep farming them off to Janet; it's really affecting them—George especially. He was so angry at me today because I'm never around. God knows what spending all that time with Janet is doing to them. She'll give them hang-ups that will last them for life."

"I understand all that, pumpkin, but think about what you are saying here. You're talking about moving away from your whole life, from your friends and your career to play happy families with someone you barely know."

"Barely know? He fucking *raised* me, H."

Heidi made a start on her mojito, conscious of the looks they were starting to attract. She lowered her voice to a hiss. "And how did that work out for you? Hm? You've got so many abandonment issues you'd rather stay single than risk a new relationship." She looks around, picking out three, four, five people she could see herself going home with tonight. "Seriously, Sam, when was the last time you even had a shag? It was that weird fucker at your work Christmas party two years ago, I'll bet, unless you've been holding out on me. And then you ghosted him."

Sam pulls her hand back and glares at her friend. "What are you, a trained fucking psychologist now? Here's me thinking you were just a shallow pisshead who shags anything with a pulse and spends all her spare cash on lip fillers because she can't stand the thought of getting old!"

Heidi's face falls, and tears form in the corner of her eyes. "What the actual fuck, Sam?"

"Oh god, Heidi, I'm so sorry. I didn't mean that. I just—"

Heidi puts her hand up. "Yeah. Don't worry about it. But I think you should go now."

Sam stands up, shocked by her own vehemence and venom. She tries to apologise, to hug her friend, to reconnect, but Heidi pushes her away, shuts her down. Sam stands there for a moment, helpless.

"H, you know I didn't mean all that. I'm just stressed. And pissed off at the world. Please . . . "

"I know, babe. And my offer of the room still stands. You know it does. But like you say, you've got an early start tomorrow, and it's going to take me a few more cocktails to process all this. We'll talk tomorrow, 'kay?"

With that, Heidi drains the last of her drink and strides across the dance floor to the toilets, leaving Sam adrift, alone. She begins to feel the weight of eyes upon her, predatory, calculating. It's the last thing she needs right now.

"Fucks sake," Sam groans, girding herself. She phones for a taxi and rides out the discomfort until it arrives.

Heidi stumbles from the nightclub at around two in the morning. Her head swims from too many drinks, and her expensive shoes hurt her feet. The night passed quickly after their set-to, and she'd done her best to push the argument from her mind. She has been the life and soul of the club, dancing to every song with wild abandon. She has kissed four bewildered twenty-somethings and got a little racy with a fifth in the bathroom. Despite the drinking and dancing, she's not in the mood to bring some inexperienced youngster back to her hotel room, though. Sam's barb about age keeps coming back to her. She decides she'll run a hot bath in her room, empty the minibar and enjoy some alone time.

Preston is not a pleasant sight at any time. At two o'clock on a Sunday morning, the streets are filled with drunken clubbers tottering along the roads. Young men openly urinate in doorways and side streets or throw up outside kebab shops. Groups of them stagger up the road, arm in arm, slurring incoherent football anthems and shoving each other good-naturedly. Chavvy girls jostle in the taxi ranks, and at least three fights break out; one of which gets seriously out of control. Two girls rake at each other's faces with clawed hands, spitting and screaming vindictively. The attending police officers break up these scuffles, and the more aggressive offenders are firmly bundled into the riot vans, restraints around their wrists.

Heidi replays the argument with Sam in her mind and shakes her head. It was far from the first time the two of them had fought. Hell, back in their university days, they would end up screaming at each other most Saturday nights, but all was forgiven and forgotten by the next day. This time, though, it felt . . . different. She knew she'd reacted badly to what Sam had said, but it ran deeper than that. It was the finality of it all. Sam wanted out, and there was nothing Heidi could do to change her mind. The simple truth was that she didn't want to lose her friend. Despite her busy social life, she kept a distance from most people. She would engage with them on social media, party with them in Soho and make the most of her nights out, but that was as far as she let things go. They never got close. She made acquaintances rather than friends, and while the intimacy of sex was never an issue for her, she'd not been in a real relationship for almost five years. Christ, she was worse off than Sam. She told herself that she didn't want to be tied down, but she was scared. Her last serious boyfriend had hurt her severely. She'd come home unexpectedly one day to find him in bed with some slag from work, and that had been that. It wasn't even like the bitch had been that attractive. She wanted a leg up and he wanted a leg over. They were the perfect fucking match. She let out a bitter laugh. "Perhaps Sam isn't the only one with abandonment issues".

"Fuck it," she says and begins the short walk back to her hotel. She'll call Sam tomorrow and sort everything out. Or try to. She'll blame the drink like she always does and smooth things over. One thing she knows to her core is that she will not allow Sam and the kids to just disappear from her life. Perhaps she can get her a job with the magazine. Sam isn't exactly a fashionista, but with some coaching and a new wardrobe, Heidi thinks she might be able to swing it. And with the additional money that'll bring, it might put any thoughts of moving away out of her friend's mind. It's not like they can't still come here on holidays. Nobody has to be hurt. Everybody wins.

She smiles, bolstered by her plan of action, and pushes on, avoiding the pitted pools of vomit. She is almost back at the hotel when two police officers step out of an alley. One of them, a tall, middle-aged man, says, "Ms Richelle? Heidi Richelle?"

Heidi narrows her eyes, suddenly cautious. Living in London, she'd learned well enough that a police uniform didn't mean that a man could be trusted. There had been too many incidents of rape, assaults and murders over the years, perpetrated by the boys in blue, and any trust between the public and the police had withered. One thought screams in her mind: how the fuck do they know her name?

The other officer smiles at her. "Nothing to worry about, Miss Richelle. But we need to talk to you about Samantha Ashlyn. It's rather urgent."

That gets her attention. "Sam? Why? What's happened to her? Is she all right?"

The taller police officer steps forward, his hands up, "Nothing like that. Sam is fine, I'm sure. We just need a word with you about her."

Heidi's concern quickly turns to annoyance. "Then why the fuck are you bothering me at two o clock in the morning? Listen, it's been a long night; I just want to go to my hotel and get some sleep. If you need to talk to me, I'll happily come to the station tomorrow afternoon, OK?"

The taller officer shakes his head. "I'm afraid that's not going to be possible, Ms Richelle."

Her world explodes in a white burst of pain, then everything goes dark.

Heidi's consciousness swims back from the depths of a nightmare. She is aware of the pain first: a burning sensation on the right side of her neck. It feels familiar, but she can't place where it came from. Then the nausea hits, great sweeping waves of sickness that drench her body in cold sweat and goosebumps. She tries to roll out of bed, her fragmented mind struggling to remember where the hotel bathroom is, only to realise she is lying on cold, damp, unyielding stone. She tries to remember what happened, but her thoughts are slippery, elusive, as if trying to remove oil from water with her fingers. A hot flush runs through her body, an acidic burn pumping pathways up from her guts. She can't hold it in, and she turns, retching onto the floor, feeling the foulness splash against her hands and the bitter flavour of bile caustic and cruel at the back of her throat.

She groans and cracks open her eyes, hoping to make sense of where she is, but all she sees is inky blackness. She feels the first cold knot of terror form in her stomach and, with effort, forces herself up into a sitting position.

Her head pounds in time to the rapid beating of her heart, and she tastes something else above the tang of her vomit. Something chemical, almost medicinal.

Was I spiked? she wonders. *What the fuck happened to me?*

She tries to piece together the events of the previous evening. She'd gone out with Sam, and there'd been an argument, she remembered that. She'd drowned her sorrows in cocktails and champagne, naturally. Dancing. Some kissing and some fingers. More dancing. Then she'd left the club and met . . . Yes, she'd met those two police officers.

Oh, fuck!

She reaches up to her neck and touches the burn mark left by the taser, wincing as her fingers probe tender flesh. The bastards zapped her, and as they bundled her into the back of their van, she had a vague awareness of some stinking rag being held over her face. Then nothing.

Heidi doubles over and retches again, but there is nothing more to bring up. It takes a few minutes for the dry heaving to pass, then she rolls away from the puddle and tries to evaluate her situation.

I'm still alive, so that's something, she thinks, though there's little solace there. All it meant was that her captors didn't intend to kill her. *Not yet at least.* Her mind fills with vivid images of what they might do to her first. She'd been raped once before, and it haunted her. The violation was more than physical. Panic rises, threatening to overwhelm her, so she tries to control her breathing. No use screaming. Not yet. *Torture?* She could picture it. *Held captive in the darkness, at the mercy of their sadistic urges, screaming and begging till they tire of me? NO! Stop thinking like that. They haven't tied me up, so I can still move. Fight. Scratch their fucking eyes out if I get the chance.* Physically, she knows that she's no match for two fully grown men, but neither of them are young—mid-fifties was her best guess, and the shorter of the two seemed pretty chubby. Out of condition. If she can cripple the first one with a kick in the balls, she might stand a chance with the other. It isn't much to cling to, but this fragment of hope gives her a little strength.

She sits up again and runs her hands over the floor. It's uneven. Rough to the touch. Not some basement dungeon, then. More like a natural formation. A cave, perhaps? The tiny, flickering flame of hope grows a little brighter. *If it's a cave, then maybe I can find a way out, or somewhere to hide at least. Perhaps even find a weapon of some kind. A big rock to smash their bastard heads in would do.*

She forces her eyes wide, straining to see something in the all-engulfing darkness, but there is no hint of light, nor of movement—nothing but inky blackness. Next, she tries to still herself and listen to what's out there. Perhaps she'll hear something that will guide her out of here. Her heart pounds in her chest, and she swears she can almost hear the blood pulsing through her veins, but when she focuses, she can make out something else: the faint musical babble of flowing water somewhere to her right.

Then, from behind her, she hears another sound. A shuffling and the click of several somethings hard against the stone. Claws, to her ears. Like a dog, but slower, more deliberate.

Heidi stifles the sob that crumples her chest, and she sweeps her hands around the floor, desperately, heedless of the vomit, until her sticky fingertips strike something solid: a rock that rolls away with a faint clack. She lunges forward, curling her fingers around its rough surface. Yes! Something solid and comforting in this nightmare.

A voice hisses through the blackness. It is female, she judges, but cracked, dry and ancient, like the wind through dead leaves.

"I can smell you, pretty . . . "

Despite her best efforts, the strangled sob escapes from her lips, and she shuffles back, away from that terrible voice, until she feels cold rock against her back—a boulder perhaps, or the cavern wall.

"I can hear you, too . . . " the voice hisses with glee, the strange shuffling, clacking sounds coming ever closer.

"Stay the fuck back!" Heidi croaks. "I've got a weapon. I'll smash your fucking head in."

A strange coughing noise erupts at that. It takes her a moment to recognize it as laughter. "I don't think so, but I'm glad you're here. I've been sooo lonely down here in the dark. And hungry, too. Sooo very hungry."

Heidi swings the rock wildly in the darkness. The noise comes closer, almost scuttling now like some hideous insect. Then it stops, and she feels the stale air move against her cheek. She swings the rock again, hard as possible, and is rewarded by a dry crack as the stone connects, followed by the slump of a body hitting the ground somewhere to her left with a groan.

"Ooooh, you shouldn't have done that, my pretty," the voice

hisses in a sing-song melody, from above her this time. "You shouldn't have done that at all."

Something lands on Heidi's shoulder and wraps itself around her body. Thin, bony limbs with sharp nails that embed themselves into her skin. Her assailant has very little weight—no more than a small child, though its reach seems too long. It's like when she play-fights with George and Julia together, all tickling fingers, if not for those terrible claws. The creature's body is dry, almost desiccated, and painfully thin.

"Will you kiss me?" it hisses in her ear, close enough that she can taste its rotten breath.

She swings with the rock again, up into the creature's ribs, but it doesn't flinch. The stone slips from her sweaty fingers, clattering away in the darkness. Heidi flings her arm between herself and the creature, her fingers grasping, trying to find purchase push it off her.

She feels a sudden, excruciating pain in her fingers, and she screams loud and long. The creature has bitten all four of her fingers off and is crunching through them with a wet, sickening snapping of bones and tearing flesh.

The pain and mounting terror give Heidi a surge of strength, and she grasps the monster, hurling it from her. Even as it flies backward, its long fingernails snake out, carving long strips of flesh from her arm and her shoulder, leaving Heidi weakened and shaking, bleeding and sore.

For a moment, all she hears in the darkness is the raw coughing laughter and the sickening crunch of its meal. Then silence.

She spins around, flailing at the darkness. She is aware of the hot, pulsing pain from her missing fingers and the slick, wet, burning sensation of the scratches on her arms, but they barely register. Her mind is focused entirely on where the creature has disappeared to.

Something lands on her, from the right this time, and she feels blunt teeth tear a chunk of flesh from her shoulder. She screams and tries to lash out at her assailant, but it drops to the ground and rips a long strip of meat from her right leg. She cries out and kicks at the darkness, only to lose her balance and land with a bone-jarring thud on the hard floor of the cave. Then the creature is on her chest. She screams and tries to prise it off as it sinks its teeth into her left breast, ripping away her nipple and around half of the soft, sensitive tissue. Heidi screams in the dark as her unseen assailant eats her alive, one mouthful at a time, until finally it finds her throat, and her cries of pain and horror turn into a wet gurgle as she falls silent.

CHAPTER EIGHT

HIS EYES SNAP open the moment the first shard of sunlight stabs between his curtains, and Noah Davis almost bounces out of bed. His alarm clock says 06:13, which is seventeen minutes early. Noah knows he'll be in trouble if he goes into his parents' room before 06.30 and he doesn't want to spoil any part of today, not when he's been looking forward to it for so long. It will ruin their fishing trip if Dad's in a bad mood, and Noah can't let that happen.

Still, seventeen minutes is a very long time to just sit quietly. It is an eternity for someone like Noah. Noah bears it for as long as he can, then starts to think his way around the problem. If he can't go into his parents' room, perhaps he can, in some subtle way, let his dad know that he is awake. After all, Dad could be lying awake right now, afraid to disturb Noah's sleep.

The boy gets out of bed and makes his way to the large wooden chest against his bedroom wall, treading as quietly as he can. He imagines himself like Scooby-Do and Shaggy sneaking on tiptoes past a ghost. Ever so slowly, he opens the chest to prevent it from squeaking, and carefully retrieves his iPad from inside. All good so far. He takes a breath then allows the lid to slam closed, scurrying back to his bed while muffled curses burst from his parents' bedroom.

His father's head pokes around the bedroom door a few moments later. Initially, Noah thought he should pretend to be asleep but spotted the flaw almost immediately. It has to appear to be real and accidental. Plus, if he pretends to be asleep, his dad might go back to bed. No. Instead, he sits upright with his iPad in his hands and does his best to look apologetic.

"What's all that banging, Noah?" his father says crossly, wiping the sleep from his eyes.

"I'm sorry, Dad," Noah says, sincerely. "I couldn't sleep because I was so excited about today, so I went to get my iPad, but my fingers slipped, and the chest banged shut. I didn't mean to."

Dad raises an eyebrow, not entirely convinced by Noah's performance. but doesn't push things any further. "OK," he says. "As I'm up now, I suppose we can start getting ready then, but you need to be quiet. We'll be in big trouble if you wake your Mum up."

Noah gives his dad a little salute and grins from ear to ear. "I'll be quiet as a little church mouse, I promise."

"Quieter than that," Dad says, then gives Noah a big wink. "Now, clean your teeth—properly this time—and get yourself dressed. I'll see you downstairs in ten minutes."

Noah gets dressed in record time and is downstairs well before his dad. He already has his shoes and jacket on by the time his father trudges down the steps.

"Blimey, you're a bit keen, aren't you? It's going to be a long day. Sure you don't want some breakfast first?" his father says with a wink.

This is a practised conspiracy. Noah's Mum went vegan six months earlier, and almost overnight, the food turned to cardboard. Noah's chicken nuggets had a weird texture now. The mince and pasta in his spaghetti bolognese tasted weird, and even the milk in his cereal was wrong. Sometimes it tasted like nuts, other times a bit like coconut. It was nasty. Noah decided it tasted like sick and refused to touch any of it. It was supposed to be better for the planet, but in Noah's opinion, it was not better for him. If he hadn't insisted on school dinners instead of packed lunch (with Dad sneaking him the odd cheeseburger), he might have wasted away to nothing.

Dad puts his fingers to his lips, and then points up the stairs. That means mum is awake and probably listening. It also means that his dad has a different plan for their breakfast. Noah can almost taste the McDonald's.

Noah returns his dad's wink. "I'm OK, Dad," he says loudly, "I don't think I'll bother with breakfast this morning. Maybe I'll take an apple with me."

They go out to the car, quietly closing the front door behind them. Noah sits patiently in the front seat while Dad retrieves the fishing gear from the garage and loads the back of the old estate car.

"Are you ready?" Dad asks as he gets into the car.

"Yep! Let's go!" he says, almost bouncing up and down in his seat with excitement.

"Oh yeah, one more thing," Dad says, producing a poorly wrapped package from the back seat. "Happy Birthday, Mate."

Noah tears the paper off and cries out for joy. His own tackle box! Complete with everything he will ever need. That means today won't be a one-off trip. It means that he's grown up enough to go fishing with his dad regularly. Every week, maybe!

He throws his arms around his dad and hugs him tightly. "Thanks, Dad! I love it."

His father kisses the top of his head. "And I love you. Shall we get going, eh? Those fish aren't going to catch themselves."

"This is a waste of fucking time."

"Good morning, Sunshine," Chris calls out to Sam as she trudges towards him, her hands stuffed deep into coat pockets. She is wearing an expression that would curdle milk.

"You're one of those annoying bastard morning people, aren't you?" she grunts in reply.

"Guilty as charged." Chris is actually beaming, the smug fucker. "Here," he says, handing her a large cardboard coffee cup. "I figured there wouldn't be a Starbucks anywhere between your place and here."

Sam takes the cup from him, the first glimmer of a smile playing across her lips. "Thanks. You have no idea how much I need this. Had a later night than I intended, and it did not go well. Did you have to go into town for it?"

"Nah, I stopped off at the services on my way. Had to fill up and grab some breakfast anyway, which reminds me . . . ." Chris produces a bacon roll from his backpack. "It's probably not as warm as it was, and I had to guess the sauce you'd want. Tomato, alright?"

Sam snatches the roll from him and crams a third of it into her mouth in one go. "Oh, God, you are a lifesaver," she mumbles between mouthfuls. "My uncle and the kids were already up and out by the time my alarm went off." Sam checks her phone. "Jesus! Seven twenty on a bloody Sunday morning. I don't know how you talked me into this. My friend, Heidi, turned up unexpectedly yesterday, and we had a bit of a girl's night out. I feel as if I've had about four hours sleep. In fact, by the time I got back to Marcus's place and finished off a bottle of pinot, I think four hours might be optimistic."

Chris walks to the rear of his car and cracks open the boot. "Well, this is the only real lead you have on your story, and it might be my last chance to prove that I'm not just some mental case. It's not like we have many options, is it? And, as far as the hangover goes, I'm going to be the bigger man and not reciprocate the care and sympathy you showed me the day we met."

Sam shrugs. "Fair enough, I suppose. What's in there, anyway? Harpoon gun? Rocket launcher?"

Chris turns to face her, holding a very expensive-looking camera with a lens as long as his forearm. "I can take a crystal clear picture from a quarter of a mile away with this. Oh, and a set of binoculars for you. Trust me, I have no fucking intention of getting any closer to that thing than I have to. It got its teeth in me once; I'm not giving it another chance."

"Yeah, well, assuming I believe a word of what you're saying, I'd feel better with something to defend myself. So, what is the actual plan, anyway? Just hang around and wait for whatever the hell this thing is to turn up and rip someone to pieces while we snap pictures?"

Chris slams the boot lid hard enough to make Sam jump. "You have a better idea?"

Sam lets out a long breath. "No . . . It's just . . . I don't know how I feel about just letting something happen to someone."

Chris puts his hand on Sam's shoulder. "It's not sitting right with me either, and maybe we're wrong. And if we aren't and there's something we can do, then, of course, we'll try to help. But there's no point in getting ourselves worked up over something that hasn't happened yet."

"Besides," she says, "I still think it's a load of bollocks." Sam cricks her back and takes a long gulp of the coffee, looking around at the landscape. The car park is a mixture of gravel and cracked tarmac, leading down to a large expanse of open water. A crenelated wall runs down to a long causeway that leads out into the middle of the reservoir. To their left, a signpost passive-aggressively notes that the buildings off on the far side of the water belong to a trout fishery and boatyard. Small copses of pine trees dot the distant hillsides. The wind whips across the open water, night-chilled in defiance of the coming day. Sam is very aware of just how close this place is to her uncle's farm. No more than five miles distant, as the crow flies. She tries to suppress the shudder that runs down her spine at the thought of Miller's Pond. When she returns to the farm tonight, she decides to see if she can persuade Marcus to take the kids away for a couple of days, maybe to Blackpool. She doesn't want them anywhere near Millers' pond until she gets to the bottom of this story and takes them safely back to London, even if Marcus has boarded it up. Maybe she should take Heidi up on the offer of sharing her suite for a few days. She needs to find some way to say sorry, after all. Marcus won't be happy, of course. He'll be hurt, but she's sure she can get him to understand. She quickly sends a text message that says. *I'm sorry, H. See you soon. Love you x*

"OK," she says to Chris. "What next?"

"Well, there's only one other car here for now," he says, pointing to an old rusting ford estate car parked at the far end. "Anglers, probably. Let's find out where they are, then sit somewhere we can keep an eye on them." He casts his eyes at the dark, slowly shifting expanse, and a shadow passes over his face. "Preferably nice and far away from that fucking water."

Sam puts her phone down and lets out a long breath. Despite the reasons for them being here, she can't help but find herself beginning to relax, perhaps for the first time in months. She'd been expecting to feel anxious about being in such close proximity to a large body of water but the railway sleepers sealing Miller's Pond closed seem to have quietened her old fears somewhat. The reservoir waters gently lapping against the shore, and the cries of sea birds as they circle the nearby trout fishery lull her into a state of calm that is in complete contrast to the hectic bustle of London life. She looks out across the flat, shimmering waters or across the open fells and wide sky and feels she can breathe again. The fresh air and coffee have even banished her hangover.

However, they've been here for a couple of hours now, and despite the peaceful surroundings, she is beginning to get a little bored. There is very little phone reception out here, and her internet connection is sporadic, to say the least. Chris seems content to sit and unwind, scanning the waters with his binoculars and occasionally picking up his camera to photograph some of the waterfowl at the far shore. She'd initially appreciated this comfortable sense of quietude. So many people she comes into contact with seem to be in love with their own voices, gabbling every single thought that pops into their heads. His silence was refreshing. Now, though, it is beginning to get on her nerves.

"So," she says. "What's your story? By the state of your flat, I'm guessing you aren't married. Any little Chris's running around?"

Chris carries on taking pictures of the wildlife as he answers her. "I was married for a while. It didn't really work out. No kids."

"Oh. I'm sorry. I shouldn't stick my nose into your business."

"It's your job, though. Right? Don't worry. It was a couple of years ago now, and honestly, it was a relief when it broke down. We just wanted different things out of life. Actually, no—we wanted exactly the same things. That was the trouble."

"What things?"

Chris gives a wry smile. "A career, a loving husband and kids."

When Sam's brow furrows, Chris tries to elaborate. "She just wasn't my type, and eventually, she worked it out. We both did."

Sam still feels confused and a little aggrieved on behalf of womankind. "Not your type? What, do you prefer blondes or redheads? Something like that?"

Chris shakes his head. "It was a bit more fundamental than that. She's lovely. Just the wrong gender."

Sam blushes as the penny finally drops. "Oh . . . shit, I'm sorry."

Chris smiles sadly. "Nothing to be sorry for. We met when we were young, and I thought I was just going through a phase. Turns out I wasn't. She confronted me about it, we agreed to part, and then she met someone on Tinder like . . . a week later. They got married last autumn. It's all good."

Sam clears her throat in a nervous, embarrassed cough. "So, have you got a partner now?"

Chris shakes his head. "No. And I'm not likely to either, at least not while I'm still in the force, for how much longer that lasts. There's a certain . . . attitude in the police service. They'd give me grief over it if it were public knowledge—mostly locker room stuff, which I can handle, but then I'd start being pushed to the fringes.

Excluded from the social stuff, and I'd find my career opportunities limited. It's a lonely life, being a copper. Depressing, really. Most members of the public run a mile when they find out what you do for a living, so I suppose I've just kept it to myself. I don't want to make things even worse."

Sam reaches across and takes Chris's hand. "Fucking hell, Chris. I am so sorry. No one should have to be alone. But, you know, maybe all this shit will work out for the best. Maybe you can find a new job where you can be yourself when all this is over?"

"Maybe, but the thought scares the hell out of me. Being a copper is all I know. It's not like I can just leave and get a job in ASDA."

"You're still young, and there are options out there. It's not too late to change things if you aren't happy."

Chris, however, has stopped listening to her. He is staring over her shoulders towards the water, skin paling in horror.

Noah grins while his dad explains the different baits and lures in the fishing box. He hardly understands any of it, lets the details pass by him rather than interrupt. Still, he listens intently and feels like he grasps the basics.

"So," his dad says, selecting a small piece of metal shaped like a fish from his box. "This is a minnow lure. Trout will be attracted by the lure and then hopefully go after the bait." He opens a plastic takeaway box, and Noah wrinkles his nose at the musty-smelling, squirming brown worms within. His dad threads one of the worms onto a barbed hook, along with a sweetcorn kernel. "That sweetcorn is the secret ingredient. Trout go mad for it."

Noah accepts what his dad is telling him as absolute gospel, even if it doesn't always make sense to him. He's been desperate to join his dad on one of his weekly fishing trips for ages, and this is the best birthday present he could hope for. It's still early in the morning, but the sun shines bright across the moors, and they have the place to themselves, which is perfect as far as Noah is concerned. He did join his dad once before, but Steve was with them too, and he brought beer. The two of them spent most of the day drinking on the riverbank, and when Noah complained he was cold and bored, his dad told him to just go and wait in the car. They got home very late that night and his mum had gone mad. It was horrible. This time though, it is just the two of them. No Steve. Just his dad 'showing him the ropes,' which is an odd thing to say, Noah thinks, because the fishing line is even thinner than string.

His dad finishes setting up the two rods—his own expensive new one and the older one he is letting Noah use. He places Noah's rod on its stand and then produces a small catapult from the bait bag. Noah just about explodes at the sight of it.

"OK, so first we'll shoot some pellets into the water to get them interested. Bring them out of hiding. Then we'll cast into that area there, beneath that overhanging tree and we'll slowww-ly reel the line back in. Now listen, Noah. It's important not to make too many sudden, jerky movements. We want the fish to think this is something natural."

That doesn't make sense to Noah—sweetcorn doesn't swim at all, so why will the fish think it's swimming? He keeps his mouth closed, though, and simply nods. His dad gets annoyed if he asks too many 'stupid fucking questions'. He learned long ago that it is best just to smile, nod and then try to work things out on his own afterwards. Unfortunately, this feels like one of those times.

"Then we cast the line. You hold the rod like this and give it a wrist flick like . . . this. See?"

The lure flies to the area beneath the tree, plopping into the water just where his dad shot the pellets. He's an expert, is Dad.

"Then we just reel it back in, niiiice and steady, and we'll do it again and again until one of the fish goes for it. Think you can do that?"

Noah nods. The line snakes towards them across the surface until it dangles from the end of the rod once more. Both the worm and sweetcorn are still in place.

"OK, now you come here," his dad says briskly, motioning for Noah to stand in front of him. "Now, hold the rod here, behind my hands, and we'll do it again. Don't try to do anything, though. I'll do the movements. You just need to get a feel for what I'm doing."

Noah grips the rod and tries to emulate his dad's movements as the line flies again. Noah tenses his arms in anticipation, jerking the rod, and the line ends up caught in the willow tree's branches.

His father shouts in annoyance. "Now, look what you've done! It's stuck in the tree." Noah wails, which only makes things worse. "Just . . . just sit down over there while I get this loose."

"I didn't mean to, Dad," he sniffs, biting back the tears. If there is one thing his dad hates more than 'stupid fucking questions', it's whining.

After a few minutes of grunting and swearing, his dad teases the line free of the grasping branches and reels it back in. He glances back at Noah and makes a visible effort to calm himself down, though his voice still carries an edge. "Right, this time, just sit there and watch how I do it, OK? Then you can reel in."

Noah nods, afraid to speak, while his dad casts the line again. It splashes into the dark water beneath the willow tree. This time, however, the float vanishes below the surface. His dad's mood changes in an instant. "Noah, look! We've got a bite!" he cries excitedly, and Noah leaps to his feet with excitement.

"I think it's a big one," he says, and begins to let some more line out. "We'll have to play with him. Tire him out before we reel him in." He grins at Noah, but then the rod is yanked from his hands and disappears into the lake.

"What? What the fuck?" he yells. He's already taking off his shoes and socks. He begins to wade into the murky water. "Never had one of the bastards do that to me before. It must be a real monster!" There is annoyance in his voice, but also excitement. This'll be a fish worth catching. One for the wall of the local, perhaps. A real trophy. As he reaches the area beneath the tree, he begins sweeping his arms beneath the water, searching for his rod.

Then, all of a sudden, he's gone.

There's just a slowly expanding circle of ripples spreading out from where he'd been standing.

"Dad?" Noah cries. "Dad, where are you?" He's uncertain. Is his dad playing a game with him? Noah runs around the bank to the willow tree, where his father disappeared. He is vaguely aware of movement from the car park. There's another car up there he hadn't seen before. A man and a woman are watching them. The woman shouts something and starts running towards him, but all Noah cares about is his dad.

He sees a shape below the water. His dad must have slipped. He's in trouble! Noah grabs a tree branch and leans across the dark, swirling water, his hand extended. "Take my hand, dad. I've got you. I've—"

A hand bursts out from beneath the water and closes around his. But it's not his dad's hand. There's nothing warm or comforting about it. The fingers are unnaturally long, spindly, like spider legs. He shrieks, long and loud, then Noah is dragged from his feet into the ice-cold water.

"Fuck! Something's happening!"

Sam's stomach lurches at the words, and she turns back to the water, dreading what she will see.

The young boy is running along the reservoir bank, calling for his father, who has vanished.

She scrambles to her feet and races towards the child, screaming, "Get back! Get away from the water!" at the top of her lungs.

She almost makes it to the boy when she sees a green hand, long-fingered, gnarled, breaking the surface to grab him and drag him in.

Sam doesn't hesitate. Doesn't even think about it. She dives headlong into the water after the boy, powers towards him and somehow manages to grab hold of his jeans.

She plants her feet on the slippery floor of the reservoir and stands upright, chest-deep in the water. Then she begins to pull on the child's leg with all of her strength.

For a moment, it seems like she is getting somewhere. The boy slips from the creature's grasp, and she drags him up to the surface. He coughs up water, his eyes wild and unfocused. She starts to walk backwards, murmuring words to calm him, stepping gently, afraid of slipping herself. Then two spidery hands seize the boy's shoulders from behind, reclaiming their prize. The boy is tugged from her again and slips beneath the water's surface. Sam grabs both of his hands and holds on with all of her strength. She screams in terror and rage. Then, taking a deep breath, she ducks below the surface.

Those spidery hands are cramming the boy into a gaping mouth, shark-wide but startlingly human. He looks up at her in incomprehension, eyes wide with shock. Sam feels the spasms of the creature's throat muscles through the boy's arms as it takes him down, swallowing him whole. The child is pulled from her hands with one enormous gulp and slides down the creature's gullet as the mouth clacks shut in a satisfied grin. She can see the squirming outline of his body in the creature's stomach for a moment. Then the monster is gone, weaving through the water into darkness.

Sam stands once more, chest-deep and chilled to the bone, too stunned to move. Hands grab her from behind, and she lets out a primal scream of terror and despair. Her nightmare is real.

She blacks out in his arms as Chris drags her from the water, and only regains her senses when she feels the tarmac beneath her feet. Then she begins struggling against him. "No! No! We have to save him! We have to . . . ." Her voice withers and dies, replaced by wracking sobs.

Chris pulls her close and holds her against him.

When she finally brings herself back under some semblance of control, she pulls away and wipes her face. "I saw it, Chris. I fucking saw it."

"Tell me. What did you see?"

"It . . . it looks like a woman. You were right. Whatever it is, it looks like a fucking woman."

CHAPTER NINE

SAM SITS IN the interview room, shivering. Her clothes are still wet, and a puddle is forming on the floor beneath her chair. There is a two-way mirror on the wall to her right, the door is behind her and her elbows rest on a cheap-looking table bolted to the floor. An ancient double tape recorder sits askew on the table. The walls are painted the sort of insipid green that is only ever used in publicly owned buildings. The floor is covered with a cheap linoleum whose original colour has long since faded. Sam has been in several rooms like this over the years, and each one has been pretty much identical, despite the geographical and chronological distance between them.

Chris had dialled 999 straight away. He only asked for an ambulance, but two police cars arrived as well, the officers bright and alert. Then, after the ambulance crew finished checking her over, she and Chris were put into separate cars and driven to Preston police station. The only concession to Sam's half-drowned state is a threadbare towel.

She understands the tactic being employed: let her sit in sodden misery for a bit before they ask any questions. Let her focus be on wanting to get out of here and warm again as quickly as possible. It will loosen her lips, encourage some honesty. However, it does seem rather an extreme way to treat a witness to double homicide, and she's not entirely sure about the legality. She'd been in shock when they put her in the squad car, otherwise she'd certainly have told them to let her go home to change before she gave a statement. Or arrest her, if they thought they had cause. Something is going on. That much she is sure of.

She gets up and squelches to the interview room door. Locked as expected. Sam hammers on it, suddenly furious. "Get in here now, or let me fucking go, you pricks. I'm catching my death in here!"

No reply comes, so she gives the finger to the CCTV camera on the ceiling, strips down to her bra and pants, and wraps herself up in the towel. A few minutes later, the door opens, and two police officers enter the room. The man looks to be in his mid-forties, a beer belly straining the buttons of his white shirt, thinning grey hair scraped over his reddened scalp. The woman is younger, probably no more than twenty-five years old. There's a coldness behind her eyes. Sam notes an overapplication of lip-filler which makes the woman look like a duck. The image makes Sam smile, and the woman returns it with gleaming white teeth. Her smile looks as fake as her lips.

The man motions for her to sit, inserts two cassette tapes in the antique recorder, and hits the record button.

"Interview with Samantha Ashlyn. Seventeenth of August, Eleven Fifteen a.m. Detective Sergeant Wilder and Detective Constable Crow present," the man says in a bored voice. Then he looks at Sam. "So, Ms Ashlyn. Can you explain exactly what you were doing at Barnfold Reservoir this morning?"

Sam doesn't like the man's accusatory tone. She smiles sweetly at DS Wilder and says, "Birdwatching."

The man doesn't rise to her sarcasm. "I see. And you were . . . birdwatching with Constable Buchanan, I suppose?"

"That's right. Quite the ornithologist, is Chris."

"And how do you know Constable Buchanan?"

"We met on a dating site: Plenty of Birds. Do you know it?"

"I can't say that I do, Ms Ashlyn. Would you please describe this morning's events? In as much detail as possible, if you don't mind."

Sam closes her eyes and tries to shut out the image of the young boy vanishing into that gaping mouth. "Chris and I were sitting, talking when we noticed something wrong by the water. The boy's father had gotten into difficulty, and the boy was trying to reach him. He must have slipped or something because he fell into the water. I ran over to help him but couldn't find either of them. Chris called 999, and you brought me here. Does that cover it?"

DC Crow went through her notes, clarifying a number of points with Sam until she was satisfied, and through it all Wilder glowered. When the officer put her pen down, he leaned across the table and dropped a bombshell. "Funny how you make no mention of how Mr Davis came to be decapitated, nor do you mention the fact you were at a similar crime scene yesterday. So, I'll ask you again . . . "

Sam leans forward herself, close enough to whisper. "So, you're admitting that the deaths are linked? Can I quote you on that?"

DS Wilders face flushes red. "I said nothing of the sort, and no, you most certainly cannot quote me."

Sam grins at the police officer. "Right, then. You have my statement, and as far as I know, I'm not under arrest. If it's alright with you, I'm going to go home now, have a long hot shower and get into some clean clothes. I'm just about done. Unless you are planning on charging me with something?"

The man's face went even redder. "I could charge you with obstruction, Ms Ashlyn."

"Do it. Then let me have my phone call, at which point I'll call my editor and have my employer's entire legal department jump up and down on your fucking head. Alternatively, open the door and get out of my fucking way. This interview is over."

DS Wilder glances at his colleague, then sighs. "Interview suspended at eleven nineteen a.m." He slams his finger down on the button to stop the tape, then the two police officers leave the room, locking the door behind them.

Sam leans back in her chair and starts to count. It's only a matter of time. They'll have to let her go.

After a few minutes, the door opens, and a tall, silver haired man in his late fifties enters. He closes the door quietly behind him. There is nothing hurried about his movements, no hint of concern or frustration. The red light on the CCTV camera winks out as the man sits opposite her, and suddenly it is Sam who is sweating. The man pushes a bag of dry clothes across the table and sits back without saying a word.

Sam drums her fingers on the table, trying to keep her face neutral as her mind whirrs. The man seems content to look at her. He's not even trying to weigh her up. He sits with the confidence of a man who has already won, while his opponent has yet to realise it.

Eventually, Sam gets tired of the game. "And you are?"

"Here to put an end to this farce. My name is Chief Superintendent Graham Shelley."

"I'm going to be as honest with you as I can, Ms Ashlyn. You have unfortunately stumbled onto an ongoing investigation.

Something which is highly classified and considered a matter of national security."

Sam leans back in her chair and cracks her knuckles. "Listen, Mister Shelley or whoever the fuck you are. It's my duty to keep the public informed, and it's your duty to protect them. But you've failed, haven't you? People are dying out there—have been dying for years, and you know it. If someone like me can work out the pattern of attacks, then you lot must have done, years ago, so now I've got to start wondering why you fuckers are just letting that thing kill people instead of blowing it to kingdom come?"

The man smiles bleakly. "I'm afraid I can't discuss any operational details with you, Ms Ashlyn, and I must ask you to cease your investigations into this matter immediately."

"And I must say 'go fuck yourself'. I am a professional journalist, Mister Shelley. I know my rights."

He shakes his head. "I'm afraid you don't understand your situation, Ms Ashlyn. National Security trumps all. I am authorised to do whatever I must to protect this country. I have no compunction in detaining you, and there's so much more I can bring to bear if necessary. Do you understand what I'm saying here, Sam?"

"You don't frighten me," Sam says, but she suddenly realises what a precarious position she is in. Nobody knows she is here.

Chief Superintendent Shelley leans forward in his chair and says in a low voice, "If I walk out of this room without the result I want, every single record of you entering this police station will disappear. You will be taken from this place, and no one will ever hear from you again. The same thing goes for Constable Buchanan. You either co-operate with me right now, or you become statistics. Does that clarify the situation?"

Sam chokes back a sob. Her head spins, and she feels like she is about to throw up, pass out, or possibly both. After a few seconds, she croaks out, "Fine. Alright. I'll co-operate. What do you want me to do?"

Shelley's eyes glint like broken glass. "It's quite simple. You are going to cease any further investigation into your story, and you'll hand over any documentary evidence you've found. You'll write an article that concludes there is no evidence of a connection between these incidents, and you will never reveal what you've found to anyone. If you agree to that, you can return to your uncle's farm and we'll call that the end of the matter. If not . . . well, I think you understand what will happen. Do we have a deal?"

Sam can't speak. Her throat constricting to the extent where any attempt to vocalise her assent will reduce her to floods of hysterical tears. So instead, she just nods.

"Good," says Chief Superintendent Shelley and pushes a clipboard and pen across the table to her. "Now, if you'll just sign this copy of the Official Secrets Act, I'll let you get back to your family."

Sam is barely holding it together as she waits for the police sergeant on duty to buzz open the door. Her head swims, thick with a soup of emotions. The horror and devastation of that morning's encounter mingles with the tangible fear that Chief Superintendent Shelley had instilled in her and a black sense of futility. And yet somehow, those disparate emotional ingredients are distilling themselves into something very close to rage. She storms out of the police station and crosses the road then hears someone call her name. She turns to see Chris Buchanan running through traffic toward her.

"Sam," he gasps, "thank God you're alright. I thought they'd—"

"They almost did," she says, cutting him off, her voice a sardonic snarl. "Had to kiss that bastard's arse and sign the official secrets act before they let me go. Otherwise, I'd be halfway to some bunker with a black bag on my head by now. What about you?"

He frowns. "The same, more or less. Plus, immediate suspension without pay and criminal charges for unauthorised use of police IT systems. That job in ASDA doesn't seem so bad all of a sudden."

Sam shakes her head in disgust. "Bastards really did a number on us, eh? Come on. Let's get a drink and work out our next move."

Chris looks genuinely shocked. "Next move? What 'next move'? Unless I'm missing something, they've properly fucked us. Your story is dead and buried, and so's my career. We don't have any next moves to make."

"Oh, balls to the story. I couldn't give two shits about that anymore, but I'm not gonna let them get away with this. We need to work out what the fuck that thing is, and where it came from."

Chris's shoulders slump. "Why? What's the point?"

Sam's mouth curls into a sneer. "Because we're going to kill the fucking thing."

They walk a little farther down the road in silence, then go into the first public house they find—a run-down dive with peeling paint on the windows and a carpet that seems to suck at the soles of Sam's shoes. The bar smells of stale beer and the lingering ghost of tobacco, ingrained in the furniture. She settles into a booth at the rear of the pub while Chris goes to order the drinks. He returns a few minutes later with two flat-looking pints of lager, then whips back for two shot glasses.

Sam raises her eyebrows as he slumps into the booth opposite her. "What's this? Are we going on a session?"

"Nope. The double brandy's to take the edge off. We can have the beer while we talk."

"Can't argue with that," Sam says and knocks the brandy back. Her face creases up, and she coughs long and loud. "Fuck, that shit's nasty", she gasps afterwards.

Chris grins, then downs his drink. "It'll do the job, though."

"There's no denying that. No more after, though. I've still got to drive home for a change of clothes at some point."

Chris lifts his lager and takes a sip. "I wouldn't worry. You'll probably be sober by the time we finish sipping this piss. So, let's start with what we know."

"As close to fuck-all as you can get."

"Not true. We know it lives in water and is working its way round on a twenty-five-year cycle. We know it devours its victims; that it attacks those victims in broadly the same places each time; that it looks more or less like a woman."

"So what are we thinking?" Sam says. "Some sort of killer mermaid?"

"I don't know. Maybe." He takes another sip. "Fuck, this is disgusting. Okay. Look, I tracked this thing back twenty-five years, but I'm guessing it's been around for much longer. I reckon we start off looking into local legends."

"There is a lady on the mount. Who she is, I do not know . . . " Sam mutters, her brow furrowing.

"What?"

She shakes her head. "Something an old woman said while I was doing my interviews. 'Ginny got him,' she said. I thought she was mental at the time. She wasn't local, though. Scouser. Liverpool's what . . . ? Forty miles away?"

"Ginny? Hang on . . . " Chris says and fishes his phone from his pocket. "I had a couple of weird emails come through yesterday. They'd gone straight into the spam folder so I almost missed them. Here, take a look."

He scrolls through the messages until he finds the ones he wants and shows the screen to Sam. The first email contains a link to the Liverpool Echo newspaper website, with a banner heading proclaiming 'Is this the ghost of Jenny Greenteeth?' along with a blurry, indistinct photograph of a human-like shape deep within a bramble thicket. The second email has an image attached to it, again a clipping from the Liverpool Echo, but far older. Men with flat caps and shovels stand around an unearthed statue of a woman, with her head tilted to the sky and her arms outstretched. The caption beneath the photograph simply states 'Ginny Greenteeth'.

Sam has to clench her fists to stop her hands from shaking. "Fuck! I feel like someone just walked over my grave. When did you say you got these?"

"One last night, the other while we were being questioned in the station. They've both come from different email addresses, and I didn't know what to make of them until you said the name."

Sam opens her own phone and types in the name 'Jenny Greenteeth' into the search engine, then sits back and takes a long swig from her drink. "Jesus, listen to this. 'Jenny Greenteeth a.k.a. Wicked Jenny or Ginny Greenteeth is a figure in English folklore. A river-hag she would pull children or the elderly into the water and drown them.'"

"That sounds about right. Is there anything else?"

Sam scrolls through her search results, "There's loads. Pages and pages of it, but they seem to mostly mention Liverpool, Cheshire and Lancashire as the most common sources of the myth."

"Liverpool is where the pattern pauses. Ten years it waits, then it works its way back up towards Preston and beyond."

"Liverpool's a big city. Where are we talking?"

Chris produces his phone and opens the map application. "There. The killings seem to start and stop around St. James Cemetery. Which is right next to the cathedral."

"St James Mount. There is a lady on the mount . . . ."

Chris pushes his rank pint away from him. "I think we need a road trip to Liverpool. See what we can turn up."

Sam reaches across the table and takes Chris's hand. "How long, Chris? Until the next one?"

"Tomorrow, if the pattern holds."

Sam drains her drink, then finishes Chris's, too. "We need to go, then. Right now. You'd better drive; I'm over the limit."

CHAPTER TEN

THE JOURNEY TO Liverpool should only take an hour, but the roadworks Sam encountered a few days earlier seem even worse going in this direction. Lines of stationary traffic snake off across the horizon. Irate motorists register their frustration by switching lanes to one they perceive as going faster, often to a chorus of angry car horn beeps. Chris drives in the slow lane, content to sit behind an articulated lorry. Sam envies him his calm. She wonders what he's thinking about. He hasn't said a word in almost forty minutes, and Sam is not enjoying the silence. Too much time alone with her thoughts. She keeps replaying the face of the young boy staring up at her from beneath the water's surface, eyes wide open in terror and hope. No matter what was happening to him, he believed he would be OK because a grown-up had arrived. He'd still had that expression on his face when that fucking thing had swallowed him. It is that hope Sam is finding hardest to deal with because she'd failed him. She'd just . . . watched as those hideous lips closed over his face, and he vanished into the creature's stomach.

Sam wipes the tears from her face and turns to Chris. "So, what's the plan when we get to Liverpool? Tool up with weapons? Local legends are one thing, but I can't help feeling we'd do better with a bazooka."

Chris drums his fingers on the steering wheel and sighs. "I found someone online while you were getting yourself sorted out at the farm. An expert in local folklore who works at the cemetery. He's agreed to meet us, and hopefully give us some idea of what we're going up against."

Sam arches an eyebrow. "Really? Did you just magic this expert up out of thin air? Seem to have found him at pretty short fucking notice."

Chris returns his gaze to the stationary traffic. "Wasn't that hard. I looked on the St James Cemetery website while you were getting changed back at your uncle's place, and there was a phone number for the guy that maintains the local history section, so I gave him a call. He said he'd be happy to meet us."

"Fucker could have just chatted on the phone. It would have saved us dragging our arses through these roadworks."

"Can't argue with that. But you're a journalist; you know what these sorts are like. He probably goes months without speaking to another human being and years between anyone actually listening. We'll get more out of the bloke if we humour him."

"Any idea who sent you those emails?"

"Not a clue. They've gone to some lengths to hide their identity, though. I tried doing a lookup of the originating IP Address for the mails and one seems to have come from the Philippines, while the other seems to have been sent from China. I'm sure the cybercrime guys could do better, but that's as far as my own meagre knowledge got me."

"OK, so instead of who, let's think about why. Why would someone send us exactly what we've been looking for? Who would even know that you're looking into it?"

Chris shakes his head and says, "I'm drawing a blank on that one as well. Someone clearly wanted to give us that piece of the puzzle, so it must be someone who knows what's going on. Maybe a relative of one of the victims who'd done their own research?"

"Or," Sam says, "someone who's involved in the coverup?"

"That doesn't make sense, though. If they are part of the cover-up, then why tell us what we are up against? For now, I think it's best to accept that someone's trying to help, but let's keep our wits about us. With any luck we'll have a better idea after we speak to this guy."

It's Sam's turn to let out a long sigh. "I suppose, but it's going to be a long fucking day. For the record, I prefer my bazooka idea."

Chris gives her a wry grin. "Do you actually know where to get hold of a bazooka?"

Despite the circumstances, Sam lets out a snort of laughter. "Afraid not. I was hoping you'd be able to help with that. Shakedown your underworld contacts and all that."

"I think maybe you've been watching too many American cop shows. Besides, I'm a police diver. It's not so much underworld as underwater contacts I make, and they all tend to be trout. Maybe the odd carp. Very little in the way of heavy artillery."

"Funny, I always think of fish in tanks."

Sam and Chris laugh far harder at the absurd joke than it warrants. There is an edge of desperation and grief to it all, but Sam feels better than she has for hours. The conversation is relaxed and easy by the time they leave the motorway and hit the Liverpool city limits.

It is almost four in the afternoon when Chris parks the car on a side street near the cathedral. The imposing building dominates the skyline, towering over the rows of red-bricked terraces. As they get out of the car, Sam feels a stab of apprehension in her stomach.

They make their way around to the front of the cathedral, then enter a sloping tunnel lined with old headstones—which opens into a walkway that snakes down into the old cemetery. Sam shivers, despite the warmth of the day. There is something about this place that she really does not like. A strange sense of déjà vu though she's never been to Liverpool before. And there's something else. No birds are singing in the trees. In fact, there is no natural sound at all, just the crunch of their feet on the gravel path and the distant hum of traffic. The cemetery itself is quite beautiful—all neat borders bedded with flowers, open patches of grass, and meandering gravel paths winding their way through—which give the impression of a park. It doesn't feel drab or dour at all. Still, Sam can feel gooseflesh breaking out across her arms, and the pang of apprehension she felt earlier begins to spike, to the point where it's an effort for her not to sprint from the place and lock herself in the car.

A chubby, middle-aged man, with grey speckles in his spiked hair, gets up from a bench and makes his way toward them. He adjusts his round glasses then extends his hand to Chris, a broad smile on his face. "Chris Buchanan? I'm William Shelley. We spoke on the phone this morning."

Chris takes his hand and gives it a short shake. "Thanks for meeting us, William. This is my friend, Sam. We really appreciate your time on such short notice."

William's smile widens, and he almost bounces in place. It's a nervous energy, excitable, akin to a child the night before Christmas. "No, no, it's my pleasure, really. I'm always happy to speak to people about the cemetery. Is there anything in particular that you wanted to discuss?"

"There were a couple of deaths in the cemetery a few years ago," says Sam. "Forgive me, I'm sure it's a sensitive topic, but we wanted to ask you about any local legends that might relate to them."

William claps his hands with glee. "Ah, you're here about Jenny! I shouldn't be surprised, I suppose. She's one of the most enduring stories attached to this place."

"Jenny?" Sam asks, feigning innocence. She's learned from experience that it's better to let people just talk unprompted in interviews, and she still feels uncomfortable about the emails sent to Chris.

"Jenny Greenteeth. The old water witch herself. Something of a speciality of mine as it happens. What would you like to know, exactly?"

Sam gives William her most winning smile. "We'd like to know all of it if possible? All of the legends, the folklore and history."

William nods. "OK, then let's take a walk. I'll tell you what I know."

The sun shines brightly overhead, casting dancing, dappled shadows as the trees sway in the breeze. The footpath meanders through the cemetery, with the cathedral dominating the skyline above towering stone walls. A large, ornate, circular building sits in the distance, and it is towards this that the trio wend their way. Despite the gorgeous surroundings, Sam's unease grows with each step further into the necropolis.

"According to legend, Jenny Greenteeth was once a woman called Jenna or Ginny Green who was part of a coven somewhere in Lancashire," says William. "When her brother grew ill and died, Jenna tried to resurrect him. From what I can gather, this did not go well, and when the rest of her coven found out, they banished her for practicing dark magic."

William sits on the stone steps of a mausoleum and lights a cigarette, taking a long drag before continuing. "It's said that she eventually found her way to the sorcerer, Manannán mac Lir, who the Isle of Mann is named after. Manannán took pity on the young witch and apprenticed her. Eventually, they became lovers, but when Manannán's wife, Fand, returned to him, she grew jealous of the witch, and Jenna was forced to flee on a boat. The sea became wild with Fand's rage, the boat capsized, and the half-drowned Jenna was eventually washed ashore here."

"Jenna was not one to languish in misfortune so, using her powers, she brought forth a spring from the rock. Before long, people built a village around the new freshwater spring—the life-giving pool from which we take our name—and they began to worship her as a deity. She lived like this for many years, building her following and powers before Fand tracked her down. The battle between them was fierce but brief. Eventually, Fand, being a supernatural being rather than a simple witch, overcame Jenna. Rather than kill her, Fand condemned her rival to eternal darkness. She bound her spirit to a wooden statue, then buried both Jenna and the statue deep within the earth. That should have been the end of her story. However, it seems that was just the beginning."

"Her community remained by the spring and continued to worship her. There were tales of human sacrifice to their goddess, and after a time, it appears that Jenna was able to escape from her prison somehow. Tales emerged of a terrifying monster, living deep within the limestone caves beneath the growing city. A woman of the water, like the mer-folk and the sirens. She fed on those who strayed too close to continue her cursed half-life. And there you have it. The legend of Jenny Greenteeth."

Sam sits in a patch of sunlight as William tells his tale, drawing her knees further up to her chest at each revelation. Knowing their enemy has not done anything to alleviate her fears. If anything, now the monster has an origin, their mission seems even more hopeless. If this creature has existed for hundreds, if not thousands of years, how can they hope to destroy it?

"Is there anything else to the story?" asks Chris. "Any more details? Talk of how to end the curse, perhaps? Or weaknesses?"

William shakes his head. "Not that I'm aware of. Sorry. However, the spring I mentioned earlier is just over there," he says, motioning to a brick alcove in the sandstone walls containing a plaque. "And when they were building the cathedral back in the early 1900s, they unearthed a life-sized wooden statue of a woman along with the remains of what seemed to be ancient dwellings arranged around it. The statue was in perfect condition. No rot whatsoever and painted bright green. I saw a photograph of it in the Liverpool Echo archives once. Then, the statue disappeared almost immediately and was never seen again. But it gives a certain flavour and some credence to parts of the legend. If you spend any length of time here, you'll begin to notice occult symbols carved into the rock at various points in the area, although some of them are pretty weather worn now. Part of the binding ritual they carried out perhaps, eh?"

He's clearly loving all this, but Sam feels like she's going to be sick. The knot of anxiety forces acid up her oesophagus, burning the back of her throat. They'd wasted an entire day for nothing more than folk tales and fairy stories. They are no wiser about how they can fight the monster, which means that someone else is doomed to meet their end in the creature's jaws. She forces down the feeling of hopelessness and despair that is threatening to overwhelm her and says, "What about this binding ritual? You say she was bound to this place, but since managed to escape?"

William laughs, "You almost sound as if you think that she's real."

Sam forces a smile, "No, of course not. I'm a journalist by trade but I'm thinking about writing a novel based on this place and the legend. I just want to keep the details consistent."

William seems satisfied with this and says, "Well, there have been reports of sightings in the area, a few deaths that have never been explained and some other mysteries. After the statue disappeared, they seem to have become more widespread, but I'd attribute that more to an increased awareness of the legend than anything else. But for your novel, I suppose you could say that the removal of the statue weakened or altered the original binding enchantment?"

"So," Chris says, "If the statue was found and buried back in the cemetery, the original enchantment could reassert itself?"

William shrugs, "I suppose so. But the statue itself has been missing for well over a hundred years. But it could work in the context of your story if you need a resolution."

Chris shakes William's hand, thanking him for his time, and then leads Sam from the necropolis back to his Range Rover.

Once they emerge from the sandstone tunnel, Sam feels her malaise lift a little, as if the cemetery itself was weighing on her, feeding on her emotional state. She squeezes Chris's hand in gratitude. "Got any more bright ideas? Or shall we see if we can find that bazooka on eBay?" Despite her attempt at humour, Sam is very aware of her voice wavering.

Chris gives her a wry half-smile. "Not a complete waste of time. At least we know what the story is now."

Sam opens the passenger door and deposits herself in the front seat, releasing a huff of exasperation. "So . . . what's the plan? Where's Jenny due to show up next?"

Chris takes out his phone and opens the map application, zooming in on a bright red pin. He shows the phone to Sam. "There you are. As far as I can tell, the next death will occur sometime in the next twenty-four hours at this place or somewhere nearby."

Sam's mouth falls open. "You are fucking shitting me? Oh my god, Chris. We have to get back there. Right fucking now."

Chris's face creases in confusion. "What's the matter? Why the sudden panic?"

"Because that pin is smack on my uncle's farm."

William Shelley watches the car screech away from the shadows within the cemetery's entrance tunnel. He waits until it vanishes around the corner with a squeal of rubber on tarmac, then removes his phone from his pocket. He selects a contact from his list and calls the number. After two rings, someone answers.

"Is it done?"

"They've just left."

"What did you tell them?"

"Just enough. Not too much. As we agreed."

"Do you think they believed you?"

"Well, they just smashed the speed limit on the way out of here, so unless they get stopped on the M6, I'd say they are on their way to you now."

CHAPTER ELEVEN

THE DRIVE BACK to Preston is torturous. Chris pushes the Range Rover as fast as the traffic will allow, but the sun is just dipping below the horizon by the time they arrive. Sam is out of the car and running toward the farmhouse before it's finished crunching to a halt on the driveway.

"George! Julia!" she yells as she throws the front door open. The lights are on in the living room, and the smell of the evening's meal still hangs in the air, along with an array of dirty dishes piled up in the sink. "George? Julia? Marcus"?" she cries, but the house is silent.

Chris enters the house behind her, and Sam turns to him, feeling the tide of panic surge in her chest. "They aren't here! Oh God, Chris, they aren't here! What if we're too late? What if something happened while we were stuck at those fucking roadworks? I . . . I . . . "

Chris puts his hand on her shoulder. "Sam, you need to take a breath. You're catastrophising. They could have just gone out to the shops or something."

Sam shakes her head and pulls away from him. "No! The truck's still here. Something's happened to them. I know it."

"Breathe, Sam. Long and slow. They could have gone for a walk. They could be playing hide and seek. Let's give the house a once over in case they left a note or something, then we'll check the outside. OK?"

She manages to swallow her fear long enough to nod, then they both climb the stairs to check the children's bedroom.

As Sam feared, there is no note nor any sign of the children in their rooms. Her iPad lies unwanted on George's bed. She leaves the room and is about to rush downstairs when she notices the office door ajar. She's never seen Marcus leave that room unlocked.

Certainly not as a child and not since her return. The light is on, and the fluorescent glare of a computer monitor turns the overhead bulb's soft yellow light into a harsher blue. She pushes the door open and gasps.

The walls of the office are adorned with photographs of her, but not from her childhood—these pictures are recent. From London. And they cover every square inch of wall space. Her eyes are drawn to a few that are not obviously long-range photographs of her. There is one of her front door. One of Grandma Janet. There's even a picture of her dropping the children off at her house. A picture of her office. A photograph of her and Heidi having a drink in a wine bar. Then her eyes are drawn to another photograph, and a hollow sob escapes. It is a picture of the car accident that killed Brian. It's close range, taken *before* the police arrived on the scene. There's Brian's body, pinned in the seat, head submerged in the stream that drowned him when the car came to rest.

She can't process her thoughts; the concept of murder too slippery and fantastical.

Marcus was there when Brian crashed. Marcus left him there to die.

Had he killed her fiancé?

She collapses in the office chair, unable to believe what she is seeing, and her eyes flick over the computer screen. The email application is open, and among the list of accounts are several belonging to her. Her personal Gmail account and work email are both open in separate browser tabs.

She forces herself to look at the emails. There's a message from the day care provider Sarah had arranged, confirming her cancellation. In Marcus's own email account, there is a series of correspondences with her boss, requesting she cover the story, with links to a Facebook group, and the offer of a ten grand cash payment if Jason helps the two of them reconcile. Marcus had paid her fucking boss off to get her here! And— *Fuck!* In another account is the winner confirmation email to Janet for the all-expenses-paid cruise she'd gone on, along with the booking receipt, paid from Marcus's personal bank account.

It was all Marcus. He's orchestrated the whole thing. Jesus! He's been manipulating her life for years to bring her to this place at this time. And now he had her children. But why?

Then she sees the purse. Heidi's Armani purse that she'd been carrying just the day before. Tucked just out of sight behind an untidy stack of IT textbooks. Sam feels her stomach drop and she pulls her phone out of her pocket with shaking hands. "No, no, no . . . " she mutters as she calls her friend. The purse begins to vibrate in time to the call tones.

"You fucking bastard!" Sam screams, and slams her fists down on the keyboard, causing several of the keys to fly across the room. Then she notices a sealed letter beneath it, addressed to her in her uncle's distinctive handwriting.

She tears the envelope open and retrieves the paper with trembling hands.

"Sam, by now, you'll have realised that none of this is an accident. For what it's worth, I am genuinely sorry for the pain you've had to endure over the years. I hated doing what I did, but it was necessary. The children are safe, and they are with me. We'll be waiting for you in the caves below the old, ruined cottage. Please come alone. It won't be safe for your friend down there. I promise this will all make sense soon.

All my love.

Marcus."

Sam hurls the letter at the wall, then sweeps the keyboard and monitor off the desk with a scream of rage.

"That fucking bastard! It was him. All along, it was all him!"

Chris has taken a step back into the hallway to avoid the flying pieces of the computer. "What do you mean?"

"Look at all this. He's been stalking me for years! Fucking my life up. He killed my fiancé, it looks like he's killed my best friend. and now he's holding my fucking children hostage."

"Jesus Christ! OK, let's take a minute. I'll call this in. We can send an armed response unit after the bastard. He won't get away with this."

She shakes her head. "We can't risk calling the police. Not after this morning. I've got to go after them right now."

Sam gets up from the chair and strides towards the door. Chris puts his hands on her shoulders to restrain her, and Sam rams her knee into his testicles, then pushes past him.

"Sam," he croaks, slumped against the door frame. "That's just what he wants you to do. You're just walking into a trap. Think, for fuck's sake!"

Sam stops at the top of the stairs, conflicting emotions tearing through her. Chris is right. Marcus will have anticipated her response. Whatever he has in mind, it depends on her running straight after her children. But the sheer maternal terror is overwhelming. "You think Shelley doesn't know about this? Think, Chris. They're in on this together, somehow."

Chris raises a hand to placate her as he struggles to his feet. "I know. We can't go the official route, but there are other calls I can make, people that I trust, so we aren't going down there alone."

Sam steps back from the staircase, a steely look on her face. "I'm listening."

Josh Fiskins turns off the stereo. "Are we sure this is a good idea?"

Mike, concentrating on rough and unfamiliar roads, lets out a long sigh. "I don't know, mate. When I saw him a few days back, he seemed like he was getting his shit together. But then there was all that stuff this morning, and now . . . I just don't know anymore."

"The boss was adamant he was persona-non-grata. And having a Chief Superintendent come down to reinforce the message this morning pretty much hammered it home. I don't like it, Mike. What's he gotten himself into?"

"I dunno, mate. Something's not adding up. I know Chris lost it on that last dive, but the alcohol stuff was a total stitch-up. He wasn't even over the limit for driving. You don't bin someone with his experience for that."

Josh returns his gaze to the countryside. It's pretty bleak out there. "I wouldn't have thought anything about it until they made us sign the official secrets act. I'm just— I'm not sure it's good to get ourselves involved in it, you know? I like my job, and the mortgage isn't gonna pay itself."

Mike slams a hand on the steering wheel. "Stow that shit. Chris has been there for us more times than I can count. I don't care what the Super says, he needs our help. If all we can do is talk him down from whatever mad bender he's gone on, we still need to go."

The car turns off the country lane onto a narrow gravel track which winds across an open field. In the distance, the twinkling lights of a farmhouse just visible behind a tall line of trees.

Mike parks next to Chris's 4X4 as a rather manic-looking woman rushes over to them, Chris trailing behind.

The old friends embrace one another.

"Guys, thank you so much for coming. I didn't know who else to call."

Mike and Josh exchange a quick glance, and Mike shrugs his shoulders. Chris is clean-shaven and doesn't smell like a distillery. It's an encouraging sign. Still, the men are reserving judgement until they hear the whole story.

The woman tugs Chris's arm. "Right, your mates are here. Can we get going now?"

Mike puts his hands up. "Hold on a minute. You've still not told us why we're here or why you had us bring all the cave diving gear."

Chris sighs. "Sorry, but I didn't want to say too much over the phone. This is Sam Ashlyn, a friend of mine."

Josh arches his eyebrows and says, "Hang on, isn't she that fucking reporter that's been turning up at crime scenes? Oh mate, fuck this. Mike and I still have a career, but we won't if our names get slapped all over some tabloid rag."

"It's not like that," Chris says. "She was looking into a story, but it seems like the whole thing was set up by her uncle to get her here. There's a room upstairs with all the evidence. Then there's this."

Mike takes the crumpled letter from him and quickly scans the contents. "So, the uncle's gone off the deep end and taken her kids into a cave system? Why call us? Why didn't you just call it in?"

"Because my name is shit right now, and honestly, I don't know who to trust at the station anymore apart from you guys. The last thing we need now is Sam and I being carted off to an interview room while the Chief Super fannies about. Not while her kids are potentially in danger. It looks like a friend of hers is missing as well."

"So, what do you want us to do?" says Josh.

Chris gives a grim smile. "I thought we'd go get her kids back, then drag that psycho prick down the station and hand him over to Serious Crimes. Unless either of you has a better idea?"

Mike and Josh look at each other. Josh shrugs, and Mike lets out a long sigh. "I'm probably going to regret this, but we're in. OK, tell us everything."

CHAPTER TWELVE

SAM PACES BACK and forth by the cars while Chris and his colleagues unload the Range Rover and move the equipment to the ruined cottage, where the cave entrance is located. Whilst she is glad to have them with her, and deeply comforting to see them working with practised efficiency, she is desperate to find her children.

"Is all of this really necessary?" she asks Chris as he carries out safety checks on a regulator. "Marcus won't have taken them anywhere that needs fucking scuba gear."

Chris puts down the equipment and puts his hand on her shoulder, only to have his hand slapped firmly away. "We don't know what we will run into down there. I know it's hard to wait, but trust me, it's better to have everything we might need to hand and ready to go than regret it later. It won't take much longer, Promise."

"Well, don't take too bloody long. I want to get the kids out before Jenna fucking Greenteeth or whateverthefuck it is turns up," she snaps.

Chris's face pales at the thought, and he looks as if he is about to throw up. Sam realises that he'd been focusing on his well-practised drills to avoid thinking about what they may have to face and feels a brief stab of guilt at the way she's treating him. To his credit, he recovers his composure quickly and hands her a wetsuit from one of the bags." It will be cold and probably wet down there. This should keep you warm. Get changed at the house if you like. We'll be done by the time you get back."

Sam glances back to the house and sees Mike and Josh walking toward them with more equipment bags. "Do you think we should tell them? About what might be down there?"

Chris shakes his head. "No. I thought about it, but they'd think we'd lost it. Better they find out for themselves. Well, better we get in and out before Jenny arrives, but you know what I mean. They're experienced police officers, and Mike is ex-military. They'll be able to handle anything we find down there."

"What if we're wrong? What if we're too late?"

Chris unclasps a buckle on his belt and draws out a vicious-looking knife. "It's not a bazooka, but it's sharp as hell. If that witch is down there, I'll cut her fucking guts out."

Sam returns a few minutes later, wearing the tight neoprene wetsuit, to find the men engaged in a heated discussion. Both Mike and Josh look less than happy, while Chris has his hands up in supplication.

"What's going on?" she asks.

"Mike and Josh think it's a mistake for you to go down there with us. They think you should stay here and call for help if things go badly."

"Fuck that! My kids are down there, and Marcus asked for me specifically. If you go charging in there without me, he might hurt them. I can't risk that. I'm going. End of story."

Mike raises his hands in exasperation. "OK, fine. Have it your way, but she's going to be a fucking liability down there. You know it. She's got no training and no experience. If she gets herself killed or injured in those caves, we can't be held responsible. It's on you, Chris. Understood?"

"I can take care of myself," Sam snarls. No one will make eye contact with her.

They pick their way through the brambled rubble of the ancient dwelling to a set of heavy iron bars on the floor, stretched across a gaping hole. The cave entrance. The gate had always been secured with a heavy padlock, back when Sam was young, but now the lock is missing, and the gate is wide open. She shines her torch into the darkness and sees a smooth rock passage leading down into the earth at a steep angle.

Mike pushes past her and begins a slow descent into the cave system, with Josh following behind him, then Sam with Chris bringing up the rear.

"It seems pretty straightforward so far," says Mike. "There's a path worn into the rock. Looks like people have been coming down here for a very long time. Hundreds of years, maybe."

Sam takes little comfort in this. The passageway is tight; two of them will not be able to stand side-by-side, and the roof is so low that Chris, the tallest of the group, has to bend his head to avoid hitting it on the ceiling. She glances behind her and sees the faint illumination of the entrance, outlined in the moonlight, growing smaller with each step. Finally, the group follow the path round to the right, and it disappears from view altogether.

Sam hates this. Enclosed spaces are one of her least favourite things, second only to large bodies of water. Her heart races in her chest as her adrenaline spikes, and she fights to suppress the rising tide of panic. She can't let any of her companions know about her feelings, though. If there is even a chance that she is about to have a claustrophobic freak-out, then Mike and Josh will insist that she return to the surface. There is no way she will let that happen. So instead, she tries to keep her mind focused on her children. She visualises them safe, back in her London flat and far away from this dreadful place. She realises that she's resented the children on some level because they reminded her of their father and the life they could have had together. Sam has spent nine years struggling as a single mother, balancing her commitment to her children with the need for a career. But she knows now that she's taken that out on the children in many ways, and the guilt floods in. Angry words spat out, when love and understanding would have been better. Raging at circumstances beyond her control while the children were within earshot. Impatience when the children's needs conflicted with her own. She vows to do better if she can only get them back, safe and sound.

The group journey in silence for what seems like an eternity. She's lost all track of time in the darkness, just putting one foot in front of the next, trying to ignore the fact that the headroom in the tunnel is diminishing; even she has to bend her head now. Then the group stops so suddenly that she almost walks into Josh.

"There's a fork in the tunnel," says Mike. "I can't really make out which way is the correct one from the wear on the floor—there are worn tracks in both directions. There seems to be a little more headroom in the left passage, but not by much. So, it's your party, Chris. What do you want to do?"

"We should probably split up and check each tunnel to be on

the safe side. If we find blockages or a clear path, we'll rendezvous back here in thirty minutes and go forward together."

"Ok," says Josh. "The left tunnel looks like it's easier going, so you two head that way. Mike and I will go right. See you back here in thirty."

"Lads, be careful, OK? We don't know what we're facing down here, and the threat in that letter is pretty specific. Keep your heads down. If you find anything come back here, and we'll work out a plan of attack together."

Josh puts his arm on Chris's shoulder and says, "No worries, mate. We'll take it nice and steady. See you in thirty." Then, Mike and Josh make their way down the right-hand fork and disappear.

Chris watches the flickering shadows on the cave wall from his friends' torches until they fade away, then turns to Sam.

"How are you holding up?" he says.

Sam manages a wan smile. "Oh, I'm just peachy. Freezing my tits off and worried to death, but apart from that, I'm great. What the fuck is that smell, anyway?"

"It's ammonia. These caves are probably full of bats. It's their guano you're smelling. Watch where you step. Bat shit is slippery as hell. It's one of the most common hazards in caves."

"Great. So, on top of everything else, I need to watch out for bat-shit. Got it."

They press on into the left-hand passageway. The going is much more difficult than it seemed back at the fork. Water trickles down the cave walls, and the previously smooth floor becomes uneven, slippery, and challenging to navigate. Sam loses her footing several times, badly bruising her knees. She brushes off Chris's offer of help and does her best to ignore the pain.

"Do you think we have a chance?" she says to Chris. "It was bad enough when it was just that fucking monster, but now we've got my uncle to deal with as well. I don't like the idea of fighting on two fronts."

Chris helps her over a rough area strewn with boulders. "I think our chances are good. As long as we don't have to deal with both of them together. A seventy-odd-year-old man I can handle. As for the other thing . . . well, let's just hope we can get the kids out before we have to deal with that. What's he like, your uncle?"

Sam lets out a snort of air. "Apart from apparently being some monster-worshipping creepy-ass nutjob? Honestly, I don't know.

I'm not sure I ever did. When I met him again a few days ago, it was the first time in years and, I don't know . . . it felt like we were finally getting to know each other. Put the past behind us. Shows how much I know. It looks like it was all just a fucking act. I don't know what to believe anymore."

Chris coughs awkwardly. "No, um. I meant—is he fat or thin? Tall or short? Some insanely fit martial arts expert or a physical wreck all set for a nursing home? I want to know what I'm going up against."

"Oh. Well, he's short, I suppose. Fit and strong from working on a farm his whole life, but I doubt he knows much kung-fu. I think the three of you will probably manage against him."

"No firearms?"

Sam exhales. "Honestly, I don't know. I've only been back here a few days. I've never seen one, but that doesn't mean much. It's a farm, so there's a good chance he has a shotgun tucked away somewhere."

They round a corner and find the path obscured by piles of fallen rocks. The way seems to be blocked entirely.

"Looks like the end of the line," Chris says. "We'll go back the way we came, and hope that Mike and Josh had better luck."

Sam's heart sinks. She begins to turn around when she sees something metallic glint among the fallen rock. She pushes past Chris then bends to retrieve it.

"Look," she says to Chris, brandishing the Peppa Pig badge. "This belongs to Julia. They came this way!"

"Alright," says Chris. "Let's go get the others, and we'll try to find a way through."

Sam shakes her head. This is the first proof that her children are down here in this terrible place, and there is no way she is leaving them for a second longer than she needs to. "You go get the others," she says. "I'm getting my fucking children back."

"Oh, for fuck's sake, Sam! We can't just go charging off half-cocked. We need to . . . "

Sam is not in the mood for a lecture. She turns her back to Chris and then starts squeezing her way past the pile of fallen rocks, ignoring her friend's pleas and the cuts the sharp stones are carving in her hands and knees. She feels Chris's hand brush against her foot as he tries to restrain her, then she feels empty air beneath her as the rocks shift, and she tumbles headfirst into the black void.

"I've got a bad feeling about this," says Josh as he clambers around a boulder.

Mike scratches at his sweat-laden hair beneath his safety helmet. "You've been saying that for the last ten minutes, Han Solo. Is there anything specific you're worried about, or are just generally being a miserable sod?"

"I dunno, mate. The whole thing seems off. We should have called it in as soon as we saw that letter. I know Chris's name is mud right now, but we could have kept him out of it. There's more than enough evidence to bring proper search and rescue teams out."

"And what would our reason be for turning up at the house out of the blue? This shit goes to court, we've got to be able to back ourselves up. Honestly, I'm starting to think Chris's paranoia is getting contagious." He stops, then. Sighs. "We'll push on a little more, then turn back. Once we meet up at that crossroads, we'll talk to the others. Get them to do what we should have done at the start and call it in."

"Do you not think we should go back now?"

Mike stops and considers his friend's words. "You know what, you're right. Fuck this. We're divers, not cave search and rescue. Let's get back to . . . Wait . . . what's that over there?"

Both men train their torches on a small, furry form tucked away behind a small pile of rocks. A plush red panda toy with Cumbria Safari Zoo written on a tag attached to it. Dirty but relatively new.

"Well, it looks like we've got something," says Mike. "You want to head back and call for backup, or push on a little more, just in case?"

Josh lets out a long sigh. "Sod it. Let's give it another five minutes. I'd feel like shit if the kids are just around the corner, and we turn back just before we find them."

Mike puts the doll back where he found it and continues along the passage. After around fifty yards, he comes to a stop and raises his hand.

Josh whispers, "What's up?"

"Not sure. Maybe there's a light source up ahead." Mike turns off his head torch and signals for Josh to do the same. The cave plunges into blackness in an instant. However, as their eyes adjust, they make out a faint glow from the passage ahead.

"OK, let's take it slow and quiet. We'll have a look and see what's what. Maybe we'll be able to wrap this up quickly."

The two police officers creep forward towards the faint, constant glow ahead of them. The tunnel begins to open up until it becomes a vast cavern, lit by green, glowing fungi. On the far side of the cave, a small waterfall spills out into a large, black lagoon. Stalactites drip down from the ceiling, meeting their stalagmite counterparts on the floor below. The formations give the impression of an enormous, fanged mouth.

Mike has never seen anything quite like it before. The closest he's come was a well-known cave dive in Japan, which boasts a few glowing fungi species. Still, it isn't even close to this place in terms of scale and sheer beauty. What a crime that this place has been kept secret these long years! Tourists would flock here from all over the world, especially given the comparatively easy access. They'd not needed any of their equipment so far.

At the far end of the cavern, the faint green glow of the fungus is outstripped by a more familiar, yellow nimbus of artificial light. Mike taps Josh on the shoulder and draws his attention to it. Josh nods in return, and the two men begin making their way around the periphery of the cave, picking their way with care. Voices can just be made out amid the roaring of the waterfall. They've found them.

Josh suddenly freezes in place and grasps Mike's arm. Mike turns to face him, mouthing, "What?"

Eyes wide, Josh gestures across the cavern, close to where they'd emerged from the passageway. Mike needs a few moments to register what he is looking at. There's movement. Something is making its way across the cave floor towards them. Slowly, sinuously, silently. It's hard to make out a shape. The colour blends in with its surroundings as it stalks towards them. Whatever it is, it does not move like a human being, nor any animal Mike can think of. It seems large—almost human-sized, although it is difficult to tell from this distance. It moves on all fours, mostly, but the rear legs are too long and angular to be a dog or any other mammal. Its movements are smooth and swift as it scuttles towards them, pausing at moments, holding so still. It's hypnotic.

Somehow insectile. And it is already between the two men and the passage they'd arrived from.

Josh tugs Mike's elbow, but he doesn't respond. He is transfixed by a mixture of horror and fascination at the strange creature coming towards them, so Josh punches him in the arm.

Mike snaps his head around, angry and scared all at once. Then he sees what Josh is pointing at.

There are more of the creatures. Lots more. They scurry from cracks in the rocks above, peep up from beneath the glassy black waters, clamber across the ceiling and down the stalactites—dozens of the things. All making their inexorable way towards them.

CHAPTER THIRTEEN

"**SAM? SAM!** Can you hear me"?" Chris yells into the darkness. He'd watched with dismay as the woman wriggled through the gap between the fallen boulders and the passage wall, reacting too late as the rocks beneath her shifted, and she vanished from sight. He has no way of knowing how far she has fallen or even if she's still alive. Mike's bitter warning echoes through his mind. If anything happens to her, if she is injured or killed, that is on him. *But, of course, if she'd done as he fucking well asked, this would never have happened!* He pushes the thoughts from his mind and concentrates on the immediate issue. Everything else is secondary.

"Sam!" he yells again, trying to worm his way past the fallen rocks. He is conscious that the noise and movement could potentially trigger another rock fall, but what choice does he have? He can't just leave her to die.

"I'm here," she calls, her voice distant and echoing. "I'm OK, I think, but my torch has had it."

Chris wriggles on, shining his torch into the darkness. It's easy to see what has occurred. At some point, the cave ceiling collapsed, punching a hole through the floor into another one of the limestone caverns below them. The ground is riddled with them in this area. He shines his torch down and finds Sam, up to her waist in water, fifteen feet or so below him.

"Are you sure you're OK?" he calls. "That's a hell of a distance. Can you move your arms and legs? Did you bang your head on anything?"

Sam shakes her head. "I'm fine. Seriously. The water broke my fall. It knocked the wind out of me, is all. I'm a bit sore, but otherwise, I'm all right."

"Jesus. Do you have any idea how lucky you are?"

Sam puts her hands on her hips and purses her lips. "Can we save the 'I told you so's for later? I get it. Now, can you get down here, or drop a rope down or something?"

Chris shines his light around the chamber. The hole Sam is in is four feet across. The section beneath is much wider, arching away from the opening a few meters on either side. "There's no way down to you, and I can't see that your kids came this way, either. Can you stay put for now? I'll go back and get the others."

"You're seriously going to just leave me down here?" Sam replies, an edge of panic creeping into her voice.

"Sam, I don't have a choice. I'll need the others to help pull you up."

"Fuck you! I can't believe you're calling me fat at a time like this."

Chris trips over his words, an age-old terror filling him. "I'm ... I'm not saying anything of the sort. I need the others to anchor the rope and help me pull you up. The dead weight of any adult is significant, and I don't want to risk dropping you."

"Chris ... I'm joking ... Or trying to. Sorry, it's how I deal with things when stuff gets really bad. Go get the others—but Chris, please hurry."

Chris leans over the gap and dangles one of his spare torches. "Here, catch this. And Sam—don't fucking move from this spot. I mean it."

The torch tumbles through the air into Sam's outstretched hands. Once he's sure she's OK, he wriggles back through the opening into the central passageway.

Chris pushes down the fear that bubbles up as he makes his way back along the passageway. He can't let it control him. The low ceiling means he still needs to move carefully but pushes on as quickly as possible. He does the calculations as he goes. It had taken them around ten minutes to make it here from the fork in the passageway. If he hurries, he can make it back in five. That will get him to the rendezvous with Mike and Josh almost ten minutes earlier than scheduled. *Damn.* He debates hurrying back to the cave entrance and retrieving the rope, but that will mean another ten minutes each way. By then, the others may have decided to go looking for them.

He decides he should waste as little time as possible, so he takes out a plastic reference exit marker and scrawls 'Sam had a fall—gone to get the rope—wait here!' on it. He places it in the centre of the junction, where it will be clearly visible.

Then he hears the screams.

Mike unbuckles his knife, and Josh does the same. There is enough ambient light from the luminous fungi to see the creatures scuttling towards them, but nowhere near enough for Mike to feel safe. The plan—such as it was—had been to keep their head-torches off to maintain the element of surprise. These creatures, whatever they are, have blown that.

Josh seems to have been thinking along the same lines, and both men snap on their head torches simultaneously, casting harsh, white light on the nightmares approaching.

The creatures look like they might have been human once. Female, every one. Lank strands of hair hang from their bony skulls. Their eyes are pearlescent white orbs, set deep in their sunken sockets. Their noses have long since rotted away, but the unnaturally large mouths hold rows of flat teeth. Their bodies are skinny, green-tinged with algae. Leathery flesh is stretched tight over their bony, naked frames, pitiful and horrific to look at. Worse, somehow, is the clicking sound they make as they near. Their fingers and toes are adorned with long, curved nails that scrape and scratch at the rock.

Initially, Mike thinks that the light might frighten the things away. If they live down here in darkness, he reasons, they won't be used to such bright illumination. He's read the Hobbit. However, the things barely register it. They are blind; their eyes are atrophied from years beneath the ground.

One steps directly in front of Josh and he gets his first proper look at it. At her. And his heart almost stops. Her stomach has been torn right open. Dried loops of intestines dangle out of ruined, mummified flesh, and yet she walks. He takes an involuntary step back until he's pushed up against the cavern wall, brandishing his knife in front of him.

"What the fuck! What the fuck are they?" he croaks.

As one, the creatures angle their heads toward him, then surge forward with frightening speed.

Mike slashes at the first one as it scurries past him, but the knife slides across the creature's bones, drawing a thin line that oozes a thick, dark liquid. The hag changes direction, leaping at him with its claws outstretched. Mike holds out his arm to ward it off and sort of catches it. He is astonished at how little it weighs.

The creature sniffs at his mouth then strokes his cheek with a talon in an almost loving movement. "Pretty . . . " it hisses. Mike hurls it away from him in revulsion.

Josh, meanwhile, is almost overwhelmed. "Get the fuck away from me!" he cries as he thrashes and kicks at the swarming monstrosities. One of the creatures falls at his feet, his knife hilt-deep in its eye. He stamps down, cracking ribs.

"Hungry . . . " the revenants almost sing in unison with a dozen voices hissing like the wind whispering through dead leaves. The other revenants fall on him, clawing, biting and tearing. Josh screams as the blunt teeth of the things rip at his flesh. He's too far gone to notice, but the bloody chunks they swallow soon start to fall from the gaping wounds in their abdomens, landing with a wet splash on the cavern floor.

Josh's screams go up an octave as he fights against the tide of revenants eating him alive. Then his screams become a wet gurgle as one of the monsters rips his throat out. More of the creatures surge from the darkness to fall on the corpse of the fallen police officer, with more papery whispers of "Hungry . . . so . . . hungry . . . tasty" joining the chorus. More wet splashes of meat falling from the gaping holes in the monster's abdomens as parts of Josh vanish down hungry gullets into stomachs that are no longer there. Those chunks are then scooped up by other creatures and crammed into their own hungry mouths.

Mike stands aghast, watching the carnage, his hand over his mouth. He can't help his friend. He can't even move. He's seen some terrible things in Afghanistan and Iraq: comrades blown to pieces right before his eyes; children as young as eight detonating suicide vests in their own schoolyards; the back of his best friend's skull was shot out on patrol while they were in the middle of a conversation. Awful things. Nightmare fuel. But he's never felt fear like this. His legs are frozen. People talk about fight or flight reactions, but the reality is that most people freeze in combat conditions, at least the first time they encounter them. Mike went through it in his first firefight during the Gulf War, but then training and experience took over. Since then, he's learned to switch that part of his mind off and get on with the job at hand. Until today.

He feels warmth bloom within his wetsuit as his bladder lets go. The feeling is almost pleasant in the chill of the cave. One of the creatures lifts itself from the corpse and sniffs at the air. "Pretty . . . ?" it hisses, and Mike realises with horror that this is the monster that attacked him before. He'd been forgotten in the feeding frenzy, but now the creature remembers the other source of meat nearby.

It stands up and turns to face him, blood dripping from the hole in its guts. "Will you . . . kiss me, Pretty?"

Mike manages to get his legs moving through a sheer act of will and begins to edge away from the suckling mass.

"Kisss . . . meee. I want to feel you . . . inssside of me."

Mike takes another step back from his stalker, but he stumbles on a small rock. The thing launches itself before he can regain his footing, and it grasps his head, wrapping its bony thighs round his midsection. Sharp claws dig into the back of his skull as the monster grinds its crotch against his wetsuit, grinning, its mouth uncomfortably wide.

It drives its face forward, sinking its putrid, green teeth into the flesh of his face, and begins chewing noisily.

He screams in terror and agony, but all this does is draw the attention of the other monsters, who fall upon him like locusts.

It takes only a minute for Mike Garland to die, but it feels far, far longer than that to him.

Sam watches the flickering light from Chris's torch fade and then vanish completely, leaving her cold, wet and alone in the cave. The water has a mild current that pushes against her legs. It is ice cold. She casts the torchlight across the cavern and spots a shelf of rock running along the water's edge in either direction. While Chris was clear about her not moving, she decides it won't hurt to be a little flexible. She can barely feel her feet, and she doesn't like her chances of mobility if she remains 'exactly' where she is for the next half hour or so.

Sam aims the torch beam down to the bottom of the underground river so she can avoid any holes or sharp rocks. She makes her way to the rock shelf, then hauls herself out, grunting with effort. The shelf must once have been at the same level as the river bottom, left behind as it eroded over thousands of years. She crouches shivering in the darkness until her wetsuit starts doing its job, warming her body with the trapped water layer. Her feet and hands remain frozen, however much she rubs them. After a while, her shivering subsides, and she scans the torch beam around the cavern, taking in her surroundings.

Moisture hangs in the air like dust and stars. The underground river lets out a gentle gurgle as it pushes on, intent on finding the lowest point, but besides that, there are no sounds at all. Sam becomes aware of, and gradually irritated by, the sounds of her own breathing. It is at once a reminder of the empty space around her and the claustrophobic weight of rock up above. The shelf she sits on is relatively flat, with few boulders or even pebbles. This tells her that the level of the underground river is not constant. It's an uncomfortable thought, and she tries to remember if any rain has been forecast. Nothing will make her day worse than a sudden, raging torrent.

She wonders how long Chris has been gone. Sam checks her smartwatch and discovers that, although she survived the fall unscathed, the same cannot be said about it. And when she fishes her mobile phone from her pocket, she discovers that it too has suffered a fatal crack, filling with water.

Of course, she has bigger concerns than an insurance claim.

"Come on, you prick. How long does it take you to get a fucking rope?" she mutters to the darkness.

Sam is not expecting the darkness to reply.

A shriek emanates from deep within the caves behind her, followed by another, then another. She thinks she hears a voice whispering in the darkness, saying, "Hungreeeee . . . !"

Sam's heart almost pops out of her mouth. She tries to rationalise what she'd just heard, but there is no mistaking it. That is a voice. Cracked, croaking but distinct. Not the wind whistling through the tunnels. Not an auditory illusion. A voice. Rasping, ancient and full of longing. As far as Sam knows, only one thing could have made that noise. Jenny Greenteeth. The monster that swallowed Noah Davis whole, the thing that has left a trail of bodies across the North West of England. The creature Sam has come to kill if she can. *But goddammit, she wanted to get the children out first!* She looks at the blade in her right hand. It is long and razor-sharp, but all of a sudden it seems utterly inadequate to the task.

And as something splashes in the water behind her— something breathy and inquisitive—she feels inadequate, too.

CHAPTER FOURTEEN

SAM HURRIES INTO the darkness away from the terrible voice. More splashes, and something like a scuffle. It is curious. For a creature used to the water, she'd expect Jenny Greenteeth to be more . . . elegant. Then she realises, it is not alone. At least three of the things are pursuing her, each eager to be first. While she has the advantage of being on dry land, she has no idea how quickly they can move in the water. If they are anything like the monster that took Noah, they can move as quickly in the water as she can out of it. *Shitshitshitshitshit.* She presses herself against the rock walls, keeping as far back from the black stream as she can.

She turns, peering into the darkness, and sees a denser black shape clamber out of the water, all too close. She raises her torch in shaking hands to pick the thing out. It's humanoid in shape. Female. Lank strands of hair stick to its scalp, and she can make out the outline of what were once breasts. The creature is wrapped in tattered, bloodstained fabric with a familiar floral print—a pattern she'd last seen Heidi wearing at the club. Only Heidi isn't in possession of the dress anymore. Sam whimpers, and the creature tilts its head like a dog. Sam picks up the pace, not entirely running but as close to it as she dares, desperate to put some distance between her and the monster that took her best friend. She races along through the darkness until, shockingly, the rock shelf comes to an end against a sheer wall. Below, the underground river plummets through a gap in the rock face. The roar of the water tells of a waterfall dropping into the unplumbed depths of the cave system.

She whips her torch beam around, desperately looking for another exit. Her pursuer is a little further behind her than it had been, cautious as it closes in. It tilts its head and sniffs the air, trying to locate its prey, and Sam now realises that it's blind. That gives her some advantage, but not much. She is trapped in the creature's domain.

Her beam flashes across the rock wall, momentarily highlighting an area where the shadows are deeper. Some fissure in the rock. It's small—only just big enough for her to squeeze into. And it may not lead anywhere. But what choice does she have? She takes off her pack, gets down onto her front, and wriggles and scrapes her way into the fissure.

The ceiling is so low that she has to keep her head on its side. There is not enough room to manoeuvre her arms properly, so she has to wriggle and push with her legs to make any progress at all. It is all she can do. Her claustrophobia is overwhelming. The unyielding rock crushes her lungs, leaving her breathless and tearful, bloodied and wild. She tries to keep her mind on what lies before her, every millimetre a hope that she will emerge into some larger cavern, find her kids and get out of this hellish place. Not on the million tons of rock bearing down on her. Not on the thought of becoming stuck and simply starving to death down here in the dark. Not on the horrific parodies of women that are pursuing her.

As if on cue, she hears the voice again, harsh, breathy and lost. "Where did you go, pretty? Where are you hiding from sweet Sheila?"

Sam freezes. Her every breath seems to be a gasp, rasping in her chest. The walls are constricting around her, entombing her.

"I can smell you, pretty," the creature hisses. Sam is sure that she feels something snag against her foot and she yelps. "Yesss! There you are! Stay right there, pretty. I've been sooo lonely. And hungry. So hungry."

Sam tries to wriggle faster, further into the tunnel, all pretence of stealth now gone. Her head cracks against the low ceiling of the tunnel, leaving her dazed, and her torch goes out. She has no way of knowing if it is broken or has just been turned off by the impact.

A bony hand tugs at her foot and Sam kicks out, dislodging her attacker for a few precious seconds. She tries to wriggle forward but discovers she's become wedged. The rock presses against her, pinning her shoulders and holding her tight. Then the hands return to grasp her ankle, digging sharp nails into her flesh.

The tide of panic that Sam has been holding in bursts through the banks. She screams uncontrollably, thrashing wildly. And in that thrashing, something tears—the wetsuit perhaps, or maybe her skin, but whatever it is, it allows a shoulder to shift and suddenly, as though being birthed, she slips through the gap, enough to use her elbows for purchase. Sam scrambles forward, desperate to put some distance between her and the slavering, sorrowful thing behind her.

"Don't go, Pretty. Don't go!"

Sam crawls forward, an inch at a time, deeper and deeper into the bowels of the earth, slickened with sweat and blood. She tries to ignore the foulness of the air she is sucking into her lungs, blocks out the pleas and the hiss of frustration behind as the creature herself becomes stuck. She just concentrates on forward motion, wriggling and pushing her way along until, up ahead, she sees a faint green glow.

Sam redoubles her efforts, the pain in her raw, scraped extremities all but forgotten in the sudden surge of hope, and she emerges at last into a vast cavern covered in glowing green fungus.

She lies by the tunnel entrance for a moment, gasping as she tries to bring herself back under control. Then her eyes are drawn to the halogen glow on the far side of the cave.

Marcus stands next to a lantern, with George beside him. Julia is cradled in his arms, unconscious or asleep, it's impossible to tell. On either side of Marcus are two men that she recognises: William Shelley, the so-called expert she and Chris spoke to in Liverpool, and Graham Shelley, the bastard bent copper who threatened her that morning. *At least the police coverup makes sense now*, she thinks, although she could kick herself for not connecting the two men's surnames before. Each of the men have their hands on the shoulders of a young boy, both around eight or nine years old. Their sons? They have that look about them. And held at bay, somehow, obedient or scared, dozens of creatures crouch. Hags. Haunting yet somehow sad.

"It's good to see you, lass," says Marcus, waving her over. "I was starting to worry you'd got lost. We've been waiting for you. For a very long time."

The creatures gather in a loose semi-circle around her, blocking any avenue of escape. Another group, over to her right are greedily scooping wet gobbets of meat up and cramming them into their mouths, lost in some kind of ecstasy. The men and the children are about fifteen meters away from her on the shore of a subterranean lake. Behind Marcus stands a life-sized wooden statue of a woman, her arms outstretched, head tilted towards the cavern ceiling. The same statue from the emails sent to Chris.

She ignores Marcus for now, can hardly bear to look at him. Instead, she focuses on her son. "George," she calls. "Come here, sweetheart."

The boy shakes his head, and Marcus pats the boy's shoulder. "His place is here with me." George reaches up and takes his grandad's hand.

The fear and horror that has been suffocating Sam turns instantly into fury. "What the fuck have you done to my children, you psycho?"

Marcus's smile broadens. "I've been educating them, is all. A bit of family history. Oh, don't fret about Julia, lass. She's just had something to help her sleep with her hot chocolate. Got a little excitable earlier. George here understands, though. He knows the right of it; said he wanted to watch. Bless him, he took to it faster than I did when I were first told. He was angry at first, but I soon talked him round. Helped him understand."

"Family history, is that what you call this? I call it kidnapping. I call it murder. I call it a cult. Shouldn't you wankers be wearing robes or something?"

The smile wavers on the old man's face, just for a moment, then the warm façade returns. "That's just how it is, love. How it's been for generations. Our family is blessed. We serve the goddess and she doth provide. Us menfolk—me, William and Graham here—we are her caretakers—the descendants of her brother, while you—and eventually, young Julia here—have the honour of being her vessel. Of carrying her spirit within you for a spell. And in return, you'll be granted eternal life. Now doesn't that sound grand?"

Sam casts her eyes around the chamber at the wizened, bloodstained handmaidens, and it hits her like a hammer. These are her forebears. "You mean, after that fucking witch uses us up, we end up like these . . . things? Crawling around in the dark? Fuck that. Fuck that and fuck you. This ends. Now!"

Sam's fingers close around her knife, and she strides forward, determined to end this. Whatever horrors she'd previously imagined, nothing compared to the fate Marcus has in store for her and for Julia. It is inconceivably grim. To live for all time in that awful state, this ghastly parody of family, hidden away in darkness, preying on those who tread near. It's the worst thing she can imagine. She'll bury her blade in her uncle's throat if she can. In her own if there's no other choice, but she's damned if she'll let him do this to her.

"The handmaidens are her honoured protectors. Our ancestors. Your grandmothers and great grandmothers, going back in an unbroken line for more than two thousand years. It's a sacred duty. A privilege."

The handmaidens scuttle across the cavern floor now to form a protective ring around Marcus and the others. There is no way she can get to the old man. Sam raises the blade and rests it against her neck as first one, then another handmaiden skitter towards her.

"I'll do it, Marcus. I'll kill myself. What will your monster goddess do then? It needs me, doesn't it? It's like a salmon swimming upstream to spawn and die. And if it doesn't have me as a host, I'm guessing that will be it, the end of the greenteethed bitch."

Marcus shakes his head. "You're far from the first to have that idea, lass, and I venture to say you won't be the last. Why do you think I've brought Julia? If you take your own life, she'll just have your daughter instead. George will father the next generation in time, and the glorious cycle goes on. Look."

Sam follows the old man's gesture and to her dismay, sees that some of the handmaidens are indeed little more than children.

"You fucking bastard. How could you do this? You raised me for all those years, pretend to care for my kids but for what? This? So you can feed us to that thing? Why would you choose *this* over your own family?"

A tear runs down Marcus's cheek, and he shakes his head. "You've got it all wrong, lass. I love you, just like I loved my sister. And I love your little ones, too. Dearly. But the goddess comes before all. She is family too, as are her handmaidens. This is our destiny. Our holy charge. Our legacy."

Sam falls to her knees, weeping uncontrollably. "Screw you, Marcus. You're just another fucking prick, destroying women's lives because it's always been that way. You think this is some sort of blessing? It isn't. It's the worst thing in the world. I hope you die screaming, you deluded, evil bastard."

Marcus shakes his head. "It hurts me to hear you say that. Truly. But you'll see things differently soon. You'll see the way, and you'll thank me for it. Look," he says, pointing to some new ripples forming on the black mirrored surface. "Here comes your mother. She'll help you to understand."

CHAPTER FIFTEEN

CHRIS ARRIVES AS they finish Josh off and then watches them turn on his oldest friend. He stands motionless, horrified in the shadows, barely daring to breathe, watching them tear Mike apart, fighting over chunks of his meat. He despises himself for his cowardice, but knows he is too late. Charging forward now would be a futile gesture. If there is anything to be gained from his demise, it is that Chris now understands that the creatures are blind. He can't do much about his odour, but he can damn well stay as quiet as a statue. It doesn't do much to calm his nerves.

Then Sam arrives in the cavern, and Chris expects her to meet the same grisly fate as Mike and Josh. But instead, the emaciated things herd her to where her uncle stands along with her children, the folklorist, and Chief Superintendent Shelley. Chris can only make out snatches of the conversation from where he stands—enough to grasp what the handmaidens are, and the role Marcus wants Sam to play.

The odds seem insurmountable. Chris counts twenty-eight of them, all sharp nails and teeth. Then there's the insane uncle and the other two men to contend with. Chris just doesn't see how he can save Sam and the kids. The odds of them making it out of there alive seem remote.

Then ripples begin forming on the underground lake's black surface, followed by a bubbling, frothing surge beneath the water. Finally, the monster from Chris's nightmares emerges from the lake. First, one long, spindly arm with a hand like a stretched-out spider breaks the surface and grasps the limestone shore of the lake. Then another arm, followed by a dripping head adorned with slick black hair entangled with weeds, emerges from the dark waters. Chris feels like he is about to pass out, have a heart attack, or both. The creature is similar to the handmaidens, but its flesh is supple, almost youthful instead of the wizened, dried-up bodies of the others. Its face could be the mirror image of Sam's, if you ignored the green slime dripping from its mouth or the rows of razor-sharp teeth. Then he notices something strange. The handmaidens all stop what they are doing and fall to their knees before their goddess, their heads down and arms outstretched. Marcus, his co-conspirators and their boys do the same, crooning words of awe and love. Only Sam stands her ground, facing up to the witch alone. Chris sees her trembling from all the way over in his hiding place, but she never looks away. Never retreats even a step. If anything, she seems to be studying it. Trying to see past the evil—searching for any hint of her mother within the monster. Chris loves her at that moment. Though the opportunity has presented itself for him to back away and make his escape, he cannot leave her to face her fate alone.

He begins making his way around the edge of the cavern, moving as quickly and as silently as possible. One kicked rock or accidental scrape and it will be all over. He has one chance to end this nightmare, and he is determined to take it. Because if the other creatures are tied to the original, perhaps by killing it, he will end them all. If not . . . well . . . at least his death will be quick.

The water witch eases itself from the lake with an almost languid, liquid movement. Its back is to Sam, but despite the green hue of the creature's skin and the tangle of duckweed across its shoulders, there is something horribly familiar about the creature's form.

It stands in front of the statue, then turns to its congregation, raising its arms to heaven to mirror the statue's pose. Sam can't help but cry out. Everything Marcus said is true. Apart from the greenish hue to the skin and rows of sharp, green teeth, she is looking at her mother's face, just as it had been twenty-five years before. She searches the creature for some trace of her mother, but there is nothing. There is no trace of the woman she loved in those cruel eyes or even in the body language or the way it moves. It's wearing her mother's skin and that is all.

"My children," it says in an awful rasping parody of her mother's musical tones. "I've missed you all so much. Being away from you for so long is the worst kind of torture. But far better than those centuries we were trapped, even though we were together."

It looks down at Sam as if noticing her for the first time, then moves to her. A dripping, spidery hand rises to stroke her daughter's cheek.

"Sam. My love. It's been so long. You can't imagine how I've missed you. How much I've longed for this day."

It takes every ounce of Sam's strength not to recoil from the creature's touch. Instead, she raises her head and locks eyes with the thing wearing her mother's skin. "You could have said hello yesterday. Introduced yourself instead of taking that little boy."

The creature smiles. "Ah, darling. You still have your fire. I wish I could have spared you from seeing that, but I had to prepare. I'll need all my strength for what comes next."

Sam's revulsion becomes rage. "And what would that be?" She spits the words.

Her mother opens her arms wide. "Why, dear, we get to be together, you and I. Has Marcus not explained?"

Sam's lips curl up into a snarl. "He tiptoed around it, but I get the drift. You're not my mother. Not really. Just Jenna Green, clinging on by your manky nails, too scared to die." She barks a dry laugh. "You call this life? Stealing our bodies and using them up? Leaving them as dried up husks? It's pathetic. It's cruel. Nah. We'll pass, thanks."

The witch's mouth spreads in a hideous grin, her green teeth glinting. "My dear," it says. "What makes you think you have any choice in the matter?" And her mouth spreads ever wider.

Sam kicks the witch in the crotch as hard as she can. "Because I have friends, you fucking monster!" she screams.

Chris seizes the moment and leaps out from behind the statue, thrusting his knife into the creature's back, over and over again until his face and arms are covered in whatever foul, black substance the thing uses for blood.

She falls to one knee, crying out in surprise; the handmaidens shriek in outrage; Marcus stumbles forward with a roar, intent on saving his goddess.

He need not have bothered. The witch twists in Chris's grasp and grabs his wrist. The snap of his arm is audible, even above the howls of the handmaidens, and a sharp shard of bone bursts through his skin. The colour drains from his face as Jenny Greenteeth turns to face him properly, sliding her other hand around his throat and lifting him from his feet.

She hurls him away with unnatural strength. He sails back across the cavern, colliding with a boulder with a wet crunch.

Sam falls to her knees, tears streaming down her face. She'd seen Chris sneaking around behind the creature and had hoped against hope he could kill it. Now his body is a crumpled, bloody heap of broken bones close to the monster's statue. She's failed her friend, she's failed her children, and now she will fail herself. What's left to her but an impossible choice? She can fight and die, condemning her daughter to her hideous fate, or she can let the monster take her and give her daughter a chance. Twenty-five years to live her life, at any rate, before the same thing happens to her.

It's no choice at all in the end.

Sam drops her knife and looks into the eyes of her mother. "Take me, then. I'm ready."

Jenna Green smiles and strides forward, grasping her shoulders with long fingers. "Thank you, Sam. I love you. And now you're going to be part of me forever."

Sam's vision blurs with hot tears, and as she blinks them away all she can see is a huge gaping throat. The creature's jaw unhinges in the same way a snake's would swallow its prey. It is then that Sam realises precisely what is about to happen. She struggles and tries to free herself, thrashing and screaming, but the witch's hands grip her shoulders tightly. Then the witch moves her head forward, slowly, almost sensuously, and pushes Sam's head into its open, hungry mouth.

Sam cries out in panic as her head is enveloped by the snake-wide gullet. She gags on the charnel stench of it and tries to scream, but she can no longer draw breath, smothered as she is in cold flesh. It takes mere seconds for Jenny Greenteeth's mouth to get down to her shoulders, then the witch lifts Sam's body, tilting her head back so gravity can do the hard work.

Sam screams as she slides into the witch's stomach. First, her head and shoulders are swallowed into the dark, tight confines of the witch's body, then her legs join her, and only her feet remain outside. Then, with a single gulp, the rest of her slides down the witch's throat to lie inside the creature's stomach.

CHAPTER SIXTEEN

PAIN IS THE first thing Chris feels as his battered body claws its way back to consciousness. It begins as a red pulse in the darkness, all-encompassing, spreading through his broken body. His head pounds hideously, and he is sure he can feel blood trickling across his face. The hot, coppery taste of it fills his mouth. He is probably concussed. The slightest movement makes his mind swim with disorientation. He tries to move his fingers. The white lance of agony that shoots through his arm tells him it's broken in no uncertain terms. Every breath feels like someone grinding broken glass into his chest, so he adds ribs to the checklist of damage. What is worst, though, is that he can't feel his legs. In fact, he can't feel anything at all below his waist. So that's his back broken too, then.

His eyes flicker open, and he takes in his surroundings. He is still in the cave. His mind struggles to piece together events. He remembers attacking the creature—stabbing it over and over with his diving knife. Then it had hurled him away like a toy. Then . . . nothing.

Oh, God. Sam!

He tries to move his head to see what is going on and is rewarded with a wave of nausea. He contains the urge to vomit—barely. Throwing up would be horrendously painful with these injuries. He gives himself a few seconds to brace against the pain then looks around again.

The handmaidens are gone, which is a small mercy. William and Chief Inspector Shelley, his former boss have also departed with their offspring. Only Marcus remains on the lake shore with George by his side and Julia asleep in his arms.

There is no sign of Sam. Only Jenny Greenteeth.

The monster is on its knees, running hands through its hair in ecstasy, or perhaps it is agony—Chris can't quite tell. The thing's stomach is swollen to unnatural proportions, and movement can be seen in the tightened flesh. It is the outline of a woman's body, twisting and writhing to be free. A sob escapes his lips as he watches his friend's final moments.

The outline of a hand presses against the stomach walls, followed by the shape of a face. Chris can see the outline of Sam's mouth stretched into a silent scream.

Another hand joins the first, pushing out, desperate to break free. The skin stretches further under this assault, becoming almost transparent and then, miraculously, the witch's belly splits open, spilling Sam out in a foul-smelling tide of green ichor.

The witch clutches at the scraps of its belly as though caught half undressed and it screams in dismay and despair. Hope surges in Chris. If Sam has escaped, there may still be a chance for them both, despite his injuries. He tries to call out to her, but all he can manage is a croak.

Sam crawls into a crouching position, then gets to her feet, dripping green slime runs from her body to pool on the floor.

She turns to face him, and grins at Chris with a mouth full of green, pointed teeth.

"I'm so glad you're still alive. I'm famished, and you tasted soooo good."

"Sam, please. You have to fight it."

"Oh, Sam's not here. I've tucked her away, safe and sound. Don't worry, though. She can see and hear and *taste* everything. Did you know that she was attracted to you? Even after she learned of your . . . proclivities."

The thing that inhabits his friend walks her flesh slowly toward him, taking its time, accentuating its hips in some horrible attempt at seduction. "What's the matter, Chris? Are you honestly saying that some small part of you didn't want to try her out? Didn't you lie awake at night, wondering how it would feel to have this body pressed up against you?"

Chris spits blood and snarls, "You aren't Sam. You're an abomination. You disgust me."

The Sam-thing pouts at his insult. "You may not like me, Chris, but I'm wearing her body. Are you sure you didn't want to be inside her? Because that's where you're going."

Chris cries out in horror and pain as the creature lifts his feet and turns his body over until he is flat on his back. He can feel shattered bones grinding around in his spine, sending bolts of white agony through his body. The Sam-thing's mouth falls open, far wider than it should be able to, and it slides both of his feet into the opening, sucking on them in a way that would be sensuous if it was not so horrific. Then the mouth closes and Chris hears, rather than feels, the bones shatter as the monster's teeth bite clean through his ankles. It holds his legs upright, both feet missing and blood spurting from the stumps. The creature chews, crunching through bone and flesh before swallowing the pulped mass that used to be Chris's feet and it smiles at him.

Marcus turns to George as Chris's screaming reaches new heights and the crunching begins "Alright, lad. It's time we went home. You don't need to see this."

George looks confused. "I don't understand, Grandad Marcus? I thought he was mum's friend? Why is she eating him?"

"It takes a lot of energy, what your mum just went through. She needs to eat to get her strength back." He ruffles the boy's hair. "Just like us, eh? You must be starving. Let's head home and get some food into us."

George tugs back, unwilling to leave just yet. "What about the other one? Grandma?"

Marcus looks down at the ruined body of his sister, and an old sorrow stabs him. He takes a deep, shuddering breath, then looks away again, closing his feelings off. She has her destiny, just like Julia. Best not to dwell on it.

The new handmaiden raises her head, shock and rage on her face. "Marcus! How could you?"

The torn husk reaches out to him, but he kicks her back and leaves her sobbing.

"Can we have pizza tonight, Grandad Marcus?"

The old man smiles down at the boy. "You can have anything you like, lad. It's a special day for us. A celebration."

George looks over his shoulder to where his mother squats, finishing her meal. "Will mum be alright?"

Marcus turns the boy's head to face front and hustles him out of the cave. He knows from experience that the goddess will need more than one sacrifice to regain her strength. Best not to be around when she finishes with the policeman. He'll bring her some more offerings when the children are in bed. He has a couple of hikers sedated nearby for that precise purpose.

He looks down at George and says, "Of course, lad. Your mum will be fine. After all, she's got the two of us to take care of her."

George smiles up at his grandfather. "And Julia!"

"Julia has a different job, lad. She's got the most important job of all, so we'll take care of her, too."

THE END?

Not if you want to dive into more of Crystal Lake Publishing's Tales from the Darkest Depths!

Check out our amazing website and online store
or download our latest catalog here.
https://geni.us/CLPCatalog

We always have great new projects and content on the website to
dive into, as well as a newsletter, behind the scenes options,
social media platforms, our own dark fiction shared-world series
and our very own webstore. Our webstore even has categories
specifically for KU books, non-fiction, anthologies, and of course
more novels and novellas.

ACKNOWLEDGEMENTS

Writing a novel may seem a solitary endeavour, but it's far from it and there are a great number of people who have directly or indirectly helped or influenced this book in some way.

My father first introduced me to the story of the Manchester Pusher in around 2015 and the more I read up on the subject, the more it intrigued me. There are at least two documentaries on this that I am aware of, both worth your time to watch. Without that seed, this story would never have happened.

I'd also like to thank Derek and Trixie Stretch, who let me write about half of this novel in their back garden , and who were there for me when I needed it. And of course, to Charlie, Emily and Luke, who taught me so much about what family really means. I love you all.

Further thanks to Linda Nagle, Dion Winton-Polak, Vix Salter, David Watkins and Kerri Patterson for providing some invaluable feedback on my earlier drafts, Ben Baldwin for yet another incredible cover, and the whole team at Crystal Lake Publishing for taking a chance on my watery little horror story.

And finally, thank you to you, the reader, for taking a chance on this book. Without you, there would be no point in we authors doing what we do. Without you we are nothing, so thank you for taking the time to read *Dark and Lonely Water*. I hope you enjoyed it.

ABOUT THE AUTHOR

Graeme Reynolds was born in England in 1971. Over the years, he has been an electronic engineer in the Royal Airforce, worked with special needs children and been a teenage mutant ninja turtle (don't ask).

He started writing in 2008 and has had over thirty short stories published in various ezines and anthologies before the publication of his first novel, *High Moor*, in 2011. He went on to write *High Moor 2: Moonstruck* and *High Moor 3: Bloodmoon* before moving on from werewolves to focus on his publishing empire and new stories that didn't involve writing quite so many transformation scenes.

When he is not breaking computers for money, he hides in deepest darkest Swindon and dreams up new ways to offend people with delicate sensibilities.

You can find him online at

https://www.facebook.com/GraemeReynoldsAuthor

@GraemeReynolds

Readers . . .

Thank you for reading *Dark and Lonely Water*. We hope you enjoyed this novel

If you have a moment, please review *Dark and Lonely Water* at the store where you bought it.

Help other readers by telling them why you enjoyed this book. No need to write an in-depth discussion. Even a single sentence will be greatly appreciated. Reviews go a long way to helping a book sell, and is great for an author's career. It'll also help us to continue publishing quality books. You can also share a photo of yourself holding this book with the hashtag #IGotMyCLPBook!

Thank you again for taking the time to journey with Crystal Lake Publishing.

Visit our Linktree page for a list of our social media platforms. https://linktr.ee/CrystalLakePublishing

Our Mission Statement:

Since its founding in August 2012, Crystal Lake Publishing has quickly become one of the world's leading publishers of Dark Fiction and Horror books in print, eBook, and audio formats.

While we strive to present only the highest quality fiction and entertainment, we also endeavour to support authors along their writing journey. We offer our time and experience in non-fiction projects, as well as author mentoring and services, at competitive prices.

With several Bram Stoker Award wins and many other wins and nominations (including the HWA's Specialty Press Award), Crystal Lake Publishing puts integrity, honor, and respect at the forefront of our publishing operations.

We strive for each book and outreach program we spearhead to not only entertain and touch or comment on issues that affect our readers, but also to strengthen and support the Dark Fiction field and its authors.

Not only do we find and publish authors we believe are destined for greatness, but we strive to work with men and woman who endeavour to be decent human beings who care more for others than themselves, while still being hard working, driven, and passionate artists and storytellers.

Crystal Lake Publishing is and will always be a beacon of what passion and dedication, combined with overwhelming teamwork and respect, can accomplish. We endeavour to know each and every one of our readers, while building personal relationships with our authors, reviewers, bloggers, podcasters, bookstores, and libraries.

We will be as trustworthy, forthright, and transparent as any business can be, while also keeping most of the headaches away from our authors, since it's our job to solve the problems so they can stay in a creative mind. Which of course also means paying our authors.

We do not just publish books, we present to you worlds within your world, doors within your mind, from talented authors who sacrifice so much for a moment of your time.

There are some amazing small presses out there, and through collaboration and open forums we will continue to support other presses in the goal of helping authors and showing the world what quality small presses are capable of accomplishing. No one wins when a small press goes down, so we will always be there to support hardworking, legitimate presses and their authors. We don't see Crystal Lake as the best press out there, but we will always strive to be the best, strive to be the most interactive and grateful, and even blessed press around. No matter what happens over time, we will also take our mission very seriously while appreciating where we are and enjoying the journey.

What do we offer our authors that they can't do for themselves through self-publishing?

We are big supporters of self-publishing (especially hybrid publishing), if done with care, patience, and planning. However, not every author has the time or inclination to do market research, advertise, and set up book launch strategies. Although a lot of authors are successful in doing it all, strong small presses will always be there for the authors who just want to do what they do best: write.

What we offer is experience, industry knowledge, contacts and trust built up over years. And due to our strong brand and trusting fanbase, every Crystal Lake Publishing book comes with weight of respect. In time our fans begin to trust our judgment and will try a new author purely based on our support of said author.

With each launch we strive to fine-tune our approach, learn from our mistakes, and increase our reach. We continue to assure our authors that we're here for them and that we'll carry the weight of the launch and dealing with third parties while they focus on their strengths—be it writing, interviews, blogs, signings, etc.

We also offer several mentoring packages to authors that include knowledge and skills they can use in both traditional and self-publishing endeavours.

We look forward to launching many new careers.

This is what we believe in. What we stand for. This will be our legacy.

Welcome to Crystal Lake Publishing— Tales from the Darkest Depths.